ADVANCE PRAISE FOR

Name Tags
and OTHER SiXTH-GRADE
Disasters

"Fun, funny, and fully heartfelt. Everyone needs true-blue friends like Lizbeth's. SuperChicken for life."

—Kristin L. Gray, author of *The Amelia Six*
and *Vilonia Beebe Takes Charge*

"*Name Tags and Other Sixth-Grade Disasters* is one of those books that explores difficult topics—divorce, a new school, being dubbed a 'weirdo'—with grace and good humor. Lizbeth's antics will make readers giggle and groan, likely both in the same breath!"

—Rebecca Petruck, author of *Boy Bites Bug*
and *Steering Toward Normal*

"Lizbeth and her pod of 'weirdos' will make you laugh then steal your heart. This hilarious and heartfelt gem is moving straight to my 'favorites' shelf."

—Lisa Lewis Tyre, author of *Last in a Long Line of Rebels*
and *Hope in the Holler*

Name Tags

and Other Sixth-Grade

Disasters

Ginger Garrett

CAROLRHODA BOOKS

MINNEAPOLIS

Carolrhoda Books®
An imprint of Lerner Publishing Group, Inc.
241 First Avenue North
Minneapolis, MN 55401 USA

For reading levels and more information, look up this title at www.lernerbooks.com.

Jacket illustration by Emma Trithart.

Main body text set in Bembo Std.
Typeface provided by Monotype Typography.

Library of Congress Cataloging-in-Publication Data

Names: Garrett, Ginger, 1968- author.
Title: Name tags and other sixth-grade disasters / by Ginger Garrett.
Description: Minneapolis : Carolrhoda Books, [2020] | Audience: Ages 10–14. | Audience: Grades 7–9. | Summary: "Twelve-year-old Lizbeth is determined to get rid of her dad's new girlfriend and make friends at her new school-neither of which turns out to be as easy as she expects." —Provided by publisher.
Identifiers: LCCN 2019034457 (print) | LCCN 2019034458 (ebook) | ISBN 9781541596139 | ISBN 9781541599345 (ebook)
Subjects: CYAC: Middle schools—Fiction. | Schools—Fiction. | Bullying—Fiction. | Divorce—Fiction. | Moving, Household—Fiction.
Classification: LCC PZ7.1.G375 Nam 2020 (print) | LCC PZ7.1.G375 (ebook) | DDC [Fic]—dc23

LC record available at https://lccn.loc.gov/2019034457
LC ebook record available at https://lccn.loc.gov/2019034458

Manufactured in the United States of America
1-47630-48110-4/27/2020

FOR JOHNNA, SANDRA AND SHARON.
SITTING AT A TABLE WITH THE THREE
OF YOU CHANGED MY LIFE FOREVER.

CHAPTER 1

I'm a big believer in foreshadowing. That's why I told the movers to put my bed right under the bedroom window. They did exactly that but hustled from the room before I could explain my plan: starting tomorrow, the first thing I would see every morning would be the sunrise. I planned to think positive, sunshiny thoughts and take control of my own story. What was left of it, anyway.

My cosplay costumes were all packed up and in storage. Mom had put her sewing machine into storage, too, so I couldn't count on getting anything new made. It's hard to have an epic story when you don't even have a character.

"Thank you again, guys!" Mom called out from downstairs as the moving truck's engine roared to life. I had to admit, the movers had been the best part of this ordeal. Darien, the strongest and nicest guy on the team, had taught me a cool secret handshake. We were basically lifelong friends now.

Mom passed my room on the way to hers. "Put sheets on your bed, honey. I'll get mine done too."

Climbing onto the bed, I reached for the blinds, then paused. We had only moved to the other side of Atlanta. My real home really wasn't that far away. It would be impossible to see my house from here, but maybe I could see something else. Maybe I could see a sign from the Universe. The Universe is always trying to communicate with us.

"On the count of three." I said this aloud in case the Universe was listening. Of course, if It wasn't, that would explain a lot about my life these days.

"One." *Show me a sign, Universe! Just a hint.*

"Two." What would the new school be like? Would I love it?

Three. I lifted the blinds.

Ack.

"There are a million disgusting fingerprints on my bedroom window!" I yelled.

"It's not a crime scene, Lizbeth!" Mom yelled back to me from her room. "Wipe them off!"

"Nothing is more personal than grime! I don't want to touch other people's finger dirt."

Moments later, Mom tossed a plastic tub of anti-bacterial wipes onto the bed.

"Thanks," I sighed, unable to summon any enthusiasm for the window now.

"I think I can find the box with our kitchen stuff," Mom said as she walked out. "Want me to whip up some mac and cheese for dinner? I'm starving."

"Yes, please! Extra butter, and if you harvest a cheese packet from another package and make double-cheese macaroni—"

"Don't say harvest," she said over her shoulder. "This is dinner, not an organ transplant." She did not share my love of scary sci-fi movies. Dad did. All of this—the move, this dumb house—was his fault.

I could hear her steps padding down the narrow staircase. A high-pitched wheeze and creak told me one of the stairs was seriously defective.

"If I get extra cheese I'll love you forever!" I called.

"Only if you take your lactase pill first," she called back. "And you'll love me forever no matter what." That was true. But I was pretty sure I could still count on that extra cheese. Mom would do pretty much anything for me. She'd always encouraged Dad and me to do our cosplay stuff together, and she had learned to sew just to make our costumes.

I pulled the stack of sheets out of their box but left the bedspread inside. There was no way I could set it on the carpet while I put the sheets on. Used carpet was creepy. This wasn't really my house, and I didn't know if mutant microbes were living in the carpet waiting to eat me alive.

We were only living here until I got rid of Dad's newest girlfriend. In the two years since he and Mom had split up, I had destroyed his prospects for finding domestic bliss anywhere else. Of course, I'd had help from our friends in the cosplay community. They were rooting for Mom and Dad to get back together, too. And they had a soft spot for kids taking on the world.

I grabbed my fitted sheet and fluffed it out, trying to get rid of the cardboard-box smell. Mom was right. I did love her and Dad, and I would love them forever, no matter what. So why did I also want to smack them right in the face with a giant pile of mashed potatoes? The impulse hit me at the strangest times and without warning.

Everything I'd found on the internet about divorce suggested that I was experiencing the stages of grief. Unfortunately, "stages" was a metaphor. It was not a venue where I might one day showcase my cosplay poses. Besides, any kind of artistic expression I attempted these days ended the same way. Even haiku.

I feel good flinging
Mashed potatoes in your face!
FEAR MY POTATO

This didn't feel like grief to me. It just felt like plain old anger.

Why was I angry with *both* of them, though? My dad was the one who'd left, the one who had already had three girlfriends in the past two years. By contrast, Mom was unbelievably awesome, never getting mad at me when I went berserk or slammed doors. She never got mad at Dad either. She just got tired, the kind of tired that sleep can't fix.

Once I'd finished putting the sheets on my bed, I grabbed the comforter and went downstairs. Plopping down on the couch, wrapped up in my comforter, I sighed and looked around. The walls were bare, except where fresh beige paint covered recently patched nail holes. Whoever used to live here had lots of pictures, I guess.

"Just when you thought beige couldn't get any more depressing," I muttered. It was the same color I'd seen in the nurse's office at my old school. A color for kids who were dizzy from the stomach flu or a broken arm. A color that had no emotion or flavor. The longer I stared at it, the sadder I got.

"You okay?" Mom asked from the kitchen. Standing at the sink to fill a pot with water, she was able to look over the counter, right at me on the couch.

I shrugged. "This house is cold."

"Grab another blanket."

"No, not that kind of cold. It . . . doesn't have any memories. Any of ours, I mean. It's blank."

Mom turned and rested one hip against the counter, nodding as she considered this. "You know what we need?" She wiggled her eyebrows.

"Absolutely not."

"A dance party!"

"Mom, you can't dance!"

"I can and I will!" she yelled, a slotted pasta spoon raised high.

She was like that. She called it being a free spirit. I suspected that pharmaceutical companies would love to market a pill to her. Millions of kids would order it for their moms, too.

I held a pretend microphone to my mouth for the commercial while she searched for her phone. "Does your mother suffer from inappropriate and ill-timed moments of embarrassing dance moves?" I said in my serious announcer's voice.

Hitting the music app on her phone, she began convulsing with shoulder shimmies. If someone didn't know she was trying to dance, they might call Child Protective Services.

I raised my voice. "If so, she may need ActHerAge, the new pill from HelpMe Pharmaceuticals."

Before I could even get through the list of ActHerAge's debilitating side effects, she grabbed my hand and forced me off the couch to dance with her.

"You can't fight this feeling!" she shouted over the music.

"It's completely out of our control!" I yelled.

"Yes! Your body knows what to do!"

"Like when I had food poisoning!"

"Wait. What?" She laughed. "Oh, who cares? We're free!"

I grabbed her phone and hit pause.

"By *free*, what exactly do you mean?" I asked. The good feeling that might have been sort of happening—and I'm not saying it was—evaporated.

Mom struggled to catch her breath. Her eyes lingered on mine with a trace of sorrow. She rested one hand on my shoulder. "Free to be happy again, honey. Free to start a new life."

My lips stretched into a tight line as my eyes narrowed. "Look around, Mom." I pointed around the house. "We're not starting a new life. This isn't new. This was someone else's. Why do you want someone else's life? I want what we had. I want *us*."

She reached for my hand but I stepped back.

"You don't get it. You never have. Without Dad, you're still you. You can just go back to being you, the person you were before Dad. But what about me? You two made me and together we made a family. Now there's no more you two, and it feels like there's no more me. Not the old me, anyway. And I don't want a new me."

Before she could say another word, I turned and marched up the stairs. My dramatic exit was punctuated by a high-pitched wheeze-creak. I hated that stair already. This house was going to be my mortal enemy; I could feel it in my bones.

I spent an hour scrolling through old pictures of me with my best friends, Camden and Eva. It was better than going online and seeing what they were doing now without me. Dad texted me asking how I was doing, but I couldn't decide how to answer, or whether he would even listen if I told the truth.

◼

Eighteen months ago, my dad introduced me to his first girlfriend, Lisa. She was a yoga instructor. He let me come with him to her class at the gym.

Rookie mistake.

"Have you ever tried meditation, Lizbeth?" Lisa asked in her singsong voice. She sounded like Elmo, if Elmo had sustained multiple blunt-force traumas to the head. Plus she reeked of lavender oil and always had green salad bits stuck in her teeth. "It might help with your feelings right now."

"Oh, could you teach me?" I asked. If you ever need to sound desperate, clench your butt cheeks together, hard. Works like a charm.

"It's easy. There are only two rules, my beautiful girl." She lifted one finger. "Sit quietly with your thoughts." She lifted a second finger. I refrained from lifting one of my own. "Do not judge your thoughts. And welcome them all. And learn from them all."

She couldn't count. Not that I was judging because

she had said that was against the rules. So I followed her advice exactly, and I got rid of her within a week. First, I welcomed all my thoughts. Second, I didn't judge them as bad or mean or devious. I guess I added the third part, which was that I acted on them.

She was horribly allergic to cats. Mom and I had never owned any cats, but our next-door neighbors had had dozens. They did rescue work for the humane society. I took my favorite sweater over to their house and asked the family to let their cats sleep on it for a few days. "Try to rub it on each cat, too, if you can," I added.

When Dad invited me along on their next date, guess which sweater I wore? Every time Lisa tried to get near me, she sneezed uncontrollably.

"She's allergic to me, Daddy!" I wailed, chin trembling. "Does she hate all children like this?"

"No, no!" she gasped. "It's just her, I swear!"

Goodbye, Lisa. Thanks for playing.

A glance at the clock on my nightstand told me it was after midnight. Wednesday was here. Most people want to move on a weekend so their kids can start at a new school on a Monday, but the moving company gave Mom a big discount for scheduling their services during the week. Discounts were important to Mom now.

I would have preferred to wait until the following Monday to start at my new school—or better yet, to turn back time a full month so that I could start at the beginning of the school year. But if time travel had been on the table, I probably would've gone back even further, made sure my parents didn't get divorced, and avoided the need for starting at a new school in the first place.

My room was pitch dark, since my blinds were closed. I'd decided I didn't want to see life from this angle. I liked my old view, from my real house.

Too nervous to sleep, I reached over and turned on the lamp on my nightstand. I grabbed my journal to review my plan.

Operation Survive Wednesday
Step One: Eat a hearty breakfast.

Before bed, I'd set out a cereal bowl next to a box of Lucky Charms. Adults always tell kids breakfast is the most important meal of the day, then they want us to eat rainbow-colored marshmallows. But then again, I've seen what those high-fiber ancient grain cereals cost, and they are not in Mom's budget. Besides, why do adults want to eat ancient grains? In the ancient world, disease wiped most people out by the time they were thirty. Speaking of which . . .

Step Two: Be irresistible.
Be the MRSA of sixth grade!

After only four hours online, I had uncovered three scientifically proven methods to make people instantly adore you.

- Smile at all times.
- Stand very close to other people.
- Ask a lot of personal questions. Pretend to be interested in the replies.

I wasn't sure how these tips worked, but science had proven they did. Not that I read the articles. If you already believe in science, why try to understand it?

Suddenly I knew what was keeping me awake. This was an important list. It bestowed great power upon me.

What if everyone wanted to be friends with me? What if people became obsessed with me and those who could not get close to me gradually withered away, like plants denied the sun? I only wanted one, or possibly two, best friends. I didn't have any plan for crowd control!

A cloud must have rolled over the moon, because even though my blinds were shut, shadows crept across my wall as I lay there, wide-eyed with worry. This unforeseen complication knotted my insides. I needed to pee.

Seconds later, I opened the bathroom door but didn't turn on the light. I didn't want to wake Mom. I stifled a gasp as I lurched onto my tiptoes. The tiles were freezing. I'd forgotten that this bathroom didn't have floor mats or rugs yet.

Quiet as a mouse, I got into position and sat—then fell straight back, hitting my head on a hard object. My butt pressed against something freezing, too. I yelled at the top of my lungs.

Seconds later, light blinded my eyes. "What on Earth?" Mom screeched.

Blinking in the strong light, I realized my error. I had sat on the edge of the tub, not the toilet.

Outraged, I pointed at the toilet. "What is that

doing over THERE?" I pointed to the tub. "The toilet is supposed to be HERE. The tub is supposed to be over there."

"That was in our old house, honey." Mom extended a hand to me. "The bathroom here is different."

I scrambled out of the tub, pulling my underwear back on and wrestling the hem of my nighty down. My butt hurt, my head hurt, and I was wide awake.

"Ugh. I'll never get back to sleep now." I threw back my head and raised one fist. "Curse you, tiny bladder!"

Mom looked at me for a long moment. "Want me to make Sleepy Tea?" That's her specialty: herbal tea with milk, plus a cookie on the side.

I shook my head. "I still need to pee."

She paused to ruffle my hair, then shuffled out of the bathroom. "Turn out the light when you leave."

I conducted my business and handled the paperwork. After washing my hands, I reached for the light switch, glancing back. That toilet was definitely in the wrong place. I glared at it.

Perhaps the Universe had sent me a sign, after all. Perhaps it was trying to warn me that nothing here would go as planned.

CHAPTER 2

"It is a little-known fact that people are more inclined to like you if they've just eaten. It's scientifically proven."

"Excuse me?" Mom asked, taking advantage of being stuck in the school carpool line to sip her coffee. The steam rolled off her travel mug, making a little puff of a cloud before it vanished. We hadn't moved forward for a while. The car in front of us honked.

"That's why breakfast is the most important meal of the day," I explained. "We all need to start the day liking each other."

We inched forward and I got my first look at Plains Creek Middle School, Home of the Plains Creek Vipers! Its dark red brick walls were pitted and crumbling. The concrete steps leading up to the chipped green metal doors were stained from red Georgia clay on dirty shoes. This place had all the charm of a high-kill animal shelter. The mascot was a lethal heat-seeking ankle-biter. What could go wrong?

"Everyone is going to like you, honey. Now will you go inside?" She reached for the door handle.

"Stop!" I said. "I need to watch the other kids as they get out of their cars." I wanted a head start on figuring out which one would be my new best friend. Someone was about to have an awesome day.

One car was holding up the front of the line, forcing other parents to drive around it. Inside the car, a blonde boy sat staring straight ahead as his mother smoothed down his hair. Only when she pinched his cheeks did he get out. He practically sprinted to the doors.

He didn't seem like a good candidate.

His mom left and the next car took its place. The dad was on the phone. When his daughter opened the car door, he didn't even turn his head. But her shirt was neon green, so maybe he was blinded by the color. She dragged her feet as she walked toward the building, looking back several times, as if hoping for something.

"This is my only chance to study the other students without being seen," I explained to Mom.

"Seems a little excessive," Mom said. "You'll see everyone when you get inside, right? Why not just wait and be surprised?"

"Mom, a decision as important as choosing a best friend demands the utmost vigilance. You know, if I had been captain of the *Titanic*, we wouldn't have hit that iceberg. Leonardo DiCaprio would be alive today."

Suddenly I got that icky feeling that someone was scoping me out. Sinking lower into my seat, I scanned the perimeter. Sure enough, next to the half-dead shrubs by the side of the building, a huge, hulking kid stared right at me. His long, shaggy black hair covered most of his face. Only his eyes blazed through the tangles. He wore oversized clothes, including an army-green jacket that looked three sizes too big. Judging by the hand-me-downs, he came from a long line of thrifty giants.

"Ready?" Mom asked. She hadn't noticed the guy.

"Where are all the normal kids?" I murmured, a sinking feeling in my stomach.

Mom laughed. I was not trying to amuse her.

"Since when have you ever wanted to be normal?"

My knees were cold jelly as the principal, Ms. Camp, walked me to my classroom. Dull green paint peeled away from the walls, revealing mustard yellow underneath. Black scuffmarks crisscrossed the linoleum floors. There was a distinct hint of mold and something else. Fear, perhaps.

Discreetly, I checked my armpits. According to the label on my deodorant, my pits were supposed to smell like an enchanted rainforest. Maybe I should have asked who the sorcerer was. The stench was suggestive of Voldemort.

"You're assigned to homeroom 223," Ms. Camp said, her petite legs hitting a shockingly fast pace. I wasn't entirely sure she wasn't a mutant squirrel. "Your teacher is Ms. Farris. She had a baby over the summer. We're lucky she decided to come back. Teachers have been dropping like flies around here."

"I can account for my whereabouts," I said, holding for the laugh, which didn't happen.

We arrived at Room 223.

I closed my eyes, breathing deeply, then opened them and forced a smile.

"Go on." Ms. Camp nudged me toward the door. "And have a great Viper day!"

A tremor of fear ran down my spine. Vipers are not known for their friendly dispositions.

◼

"So, you're my new teacher?" I asked. Ms. Farris was busy scribbling something in a planner and didn't look up. I wanted to make a great first impression, mainly because an entire classroom of kids was staring at my back. When I turned around and stared into their faces for the first time, I would choose my best friend(s). And, if you recall, it was mission critical that I choose my best friend(s) immediately. With great power comes great responsibility.

Mrs. Farris looked with one eye closed. "Who are you?"

"A student ready to learn, ma'am!"

That got a reaction, at least. The kids behind me snickered.

Ms. Farris muttered wildly. "It's today? It's today. New student today. They told me about this." Still muttering, she opened her desk drawer, rummaging around inside until she pulled out a name tag.

It was ugly red, with white block letters above a blank white space.

As if I was incapable of introducing myself! Other than laser battle noises and death spirals, introductions were what I did best.

Ms. Farris held it out to me, but I politely refused. "No, thank you."

She looked up, her eyes focusing on my face for the first time. "I'm sorry I was unprepared. I'm sleep-deprived right now. I need you to wear this at all times until my baby sleeps through the night or I learn your name, whichever happens first."

"Stickers are for bananas." Seeing her eyes darken, I added, "Ma'am." Her expression didn't soften. "Hey, I have a great idea! If you don't mind, I can just introduce myself to you on a daily basis." I stuck out my hand for her to shake. "I'm Lizbeth Murphy."

"Okay," she sighed. "I see how this is going to go." Moving papers on her desk, she found a marker. "Do you spell Lizbeth with a *Z*?"

"Among other letters, yes." I paused, holding for

the laugh, but somehow feeling like I was slipping down a wet muddy hill.

She put down her marker and stared, hard. "Exactly how much trouble am I going to have with you, Lizbeth-among-other-letters?"

I had faced tougher audiences. At a nursing home last year, I performed a monologue from *Fullmetal Alchemist* and someone died during the performance. I thought the man had dozed off. A nurse told me not to take this personally, but the timing was suspicious. "None, ma'am."

She filled out the name tag and handed it to me. Dutifully, I peeled the tag away from the paper backing and affixed the label to my shirt as I turned back toward my classmates. Then I saw the tag was crooked, so I tried to peel it back off, but it must have been made with superglue. I tugged at it so hard that my shirt lifted up, exposing my belly button. Which made everyone giggle again.

Ms. Farris clapped once and raised her voice. "We have a new student joining us. Her name is Lizbeth."

Dropping my hands to my sides and taking a deep breath, I tried to focus as I surveyed my classmates for the first time. Who was about to have the best year of their life?

The desks were all in groups of four, pushed together so the students faced each other, like little floating islands. I tried to work quickly.

Scanning each group for a welcoming face, I found none. There was plenty of interest in their expressions, though. Or was it disgust? It looked like disgust. I hadn't planned for that. I hadn't even *done* anything yet.

Ms. Farris took a gulp of coffee before pressing her fingertips into her eye sockets.

I cleared my throat. She pointed, without even opening her eyes. "That pod in the back, in the farthest corner. It's the only one with an open seat."

The room grew still. No one moved, unless you count their eyes tracking my progress toward the back desk.

I heard someone swallow, followed by some whispers:

"She has to sit with the Weirdos."

"They finally have a fourth pod member."

"We'll never have to partner up with them again."

"This is going to be the best year of our lives."

People often underestimate sweet and cheerful girls. They do so at their peril. Cheerful sweetness is as powerful as rocket fuel when used correctly.

Dad was still at the beginning of this learning curve when he started dating his second girlfriend. He was only a bit nervous about introducing me to Margee.

"No drama, okay, peaches?" he said. Being a Georgia girl meant I automatically had this nickname. Georgians are wild about peaches. In the city of Atlanta, there are seventy-one streets named Peachtree, for example. Margee should have known that there was no escape from peaches.

I recognized her immediately. She had participated in, but not won, the Klingon beauty pageant at last year's Dragon Con. A Klingon beauty pageant is not like other beauty pageants. Klingons are not beautiful, except maybe to other Klingons. If you want to win the title of Miss Klingon, you've got to have lizard skin and forehead nobs.

Margee remembered me, too. "Ohmygoodness! Hello, Gamora!"

Last year, I was Gamora and my dad was Star Lord. After the beauty pageant, Dad and Margee had stopped to talk. Margee had offered to teach me how to layer several shades of green to create the right skin tone for Gamora. Dad said I would love to learn. Neither adult waited for my response.

Margee had promptly spread her cosmetics kit across a folding chair and given me an impromptu special effects makeup lesson. Her secret finishing touch was a final dab of bright gold highlight across the cheeks and nose that really brought my Gamora to life. Unfortunately, by the time I got my Gamora just right, Dad had gotten Margee's number.

The next time we met, I played nice while my dad drove us to a local coffee shop, which had a guitar player on Saturday afternoons and served my favorite iced coffee, piled high with whipped cream.

I ordered extra whipped cream. I had a plan, compliments of my online friends in the cosplay world. If people think you're brainstorming a script, they'll give you all kinds of ideas. Cosplayers are reliably awesome like that.

When the guitar player launched into his happy-clappy set of songs, I nudged Dad. "You love dancing to this one!"

He shook his head, his cheeks turning red. "In the living room, yeah. Not in public!"

Margee beamed. "Oh, let's dance! All of us, let's just get up and dance!"

I patted my belly, laughing. "Did you see all the whipped cream I just ate? I'll throw up if I move right now!"

Completely unaware of the danger she was in, she grabbed Dad and they moved a few feet away, dancing and giggling like kids.

I reached for her purse.

Later, when I wanted another drink, Dad handed me his wallet, too absorbed in his conversation with Margee to get up and pay. It's almost as if I knew he would do that.

When it was time to go, Dad pulled out his wallet to drop a dollar into the guitar player's tip jar. Margee's credit cards fell out in a clatter.

"Dad!" I gasped. "The conditions of your parole were very clear!" I turned to Margee. "Don't be too hard on yourself. He had me fooled, too. I thought he actually liked you."

"That's not funny!" Dad warned me. He turned to Margee. "I'm sorry. She's got a wild imagination. She plays pranks on all my girlfriends."

"*All* your girlfriends?" Margee asked, her tone ice-cold.

"Not all of them!" I protested, widening my eyes, then leaning toward Margee as if to confide a secret. "There's one he actually really likes. He won't let me do anything to her. He says she's special."

Goodbye, Margee. Thanks for playing.

But soon afterward, Dad upgraded my opponent. His new girlfriend's name is Claire. She's an attorney who wears boring beige clothes and always has coffee breath. I cannot stand her.

So far, she's survived every attempt I've made to terminate their relationship. She's the cockroach of girlfriends. Cockroaches are nearly impossible to get rid of. My online research says the only tactic that consistently works is the ol' surprise-and-smash. But I can't whack Claire over the head with a shoe.

I've tried, of course. She's just too tall.

▧

"Pods are for life," a kid murmured as I walked past. "Like ocean mammals."

My heart beat faster even as my steps became slower, like in a dream where you want to run but everything is in slow motion. My sneakers made the tiniest squeak against the linoleum, the sound rico-cheting off the walls.

A mass of army green swiveled as the giant stalker kid turned to face me. The empty seat was next to him, on his right. I glanced at my other two pod-mates. The hair-smoothed, cheek-pinched momma's boy was one. The girl with the neon-green shirt, whose father had a phone attached to his ear, was the other.

My friends had just been assigned to me. THIS WAS NOT MY PLAN.

The giant guy reached over to the empty chair, pushing it away from the desk. The chair legs screeched against the floor. The other two kids stared at me, their eyes wide with interest.

As I sat, the girl flashed her pod-mates some kind of secret sign that I pretended not to see. The big guy was breathing through his mouth, silently watching me. The momma's boy rubbed his chin thought-fully, squinting. The girl withdrew a piece of note-book paper from her desk as Ms. Farris walked to the board to begin the first lesson of the day.

No one paid any attention to the lesson; all the students were watching me, to see how I would react to my pod-mates. I tried to keep my eyes on my own desk or on the board. Why were the Weirdos so bad?

Why did no one want to be friends with them?

The details didn't matter right now, though. It was clear that if I sat here, no one would want to be friends with *me*.

The girl across from me began frantically writing on her paper, then stared at it, crumpled it, and stuffed it back in her desk. When she reached for a second piece of paper, the giant guy slowly shook his head. She frowned, her shoulders slumping. The giant guy turned his gaze toward the momma's boy, repeating the same silent warning. The momma's boy shrugged as if to say he hadn't done anything.

Too much had gone into my plan. I couldn't let the dream die now.

I glanced at the clock. I just had to survive until lunch. At lunch, I would spring into action and correct this injustice. I'd get Ms. Farris to reassign me to another pod, and there I absolutely would find my best friend(s) for life.

Someday we'd laugh about this.

After auto-piloting us through science, language arts, and social studies, Ms. Farris marched us to the gym for the tail end of a six-week-long PE unit and excused herself right before the lunch bell, thwarting my intention to ask her for a new seat assignment.

However, I had made the decision. I had found my Chosen One, my new best friend. I couldn't wait to tell her!

We followed the gym teacher down the hall to the cafeteria. This could still turn out to be the Best First Day Ever, if it ended well. It's like the old cosplay clichés: Sad origin story = cool superhero. Heartbreaking beginning = megacool ending. It is a law of stage and screen that there must always be a correlation between suckage and awesomeness. I was just on the wrong side of that equation at the moment.

As we marched single-file to the cafeteria, I cut the line and stood behind my new best friend. She looked a lot like my best friends back home, Eva and Camden. Both were tall with long, stick-straight hair, just like this girl. I felt comfortable with her already.

When I used to stand in between Eva and Camden, we joked that we looked like an ice cream sandwich: two thin wafers on the outside and a nutty center. They had stopped eating ice cream lately, though, so we didn't joke about that anymore. They seemed more worried about calories than taste these days.

I swept aside my thoughts of Eva and Camden, focusing instead on my new best friend. Perhaps she could explain who the Weirdos were. And that conversation would spark a bond between us that would last for the rest of our lives. I was beginning to really love our story. Gosh, I had so much to tell her.

"Hi," I blurted out, matching her pace.

She whipped around, almost knocking me off balance. "What are you doing?"

"Just letting you know that I'm here for you." According to my research, she would come to find this reassuring. I smiled brightly.

She scowled and nudged the girl in front of her, who nudged another kid, and suddenly all the girls at the front of the line were talking, pointing back at me. From the whispers, I came to understand that my new best friend was named Hailey.

"No talking in the halls!" the gym teacher screeched. Her eyes swept up and down the line like a searchlight. Several of the girls pointed at me and the teacher frowned, zeroing in on her target. "You're the new girl, aren't you?"

I accidently stopped smiling.

"If you don't want a discipline slip, then no talk-ing in the halls."

I have never taken home a bad behavior report, not even in pre-k. My record is perfect. Unable to talk, I saluted. Turns out, that was equally bad. The teacher gave me the stink-eye, and I was pretty sure she planned on reporting this to Ms. Farris . . .

Craning my neck to see into the cafeteria, I braced myself for what came next. The one worry I hadn't prepared for awaited me just ahead.

CHAPTER 3

For the first time in my life, I had to get the school lunch using the free-and-reduced-price lunch program. How was it possible that Mom was working harder than ever and had less money now? Nothing about my parents' divorce made any sense.

"You okay?"

I turned to see the neon girl from my pod behind me. I had to keep moving forward, but I was panicking.

"School lunches are funded by the federal government," I said. "The very same government that creates weapons of mass destruction." I get chatty when nervous. "Why isn't anyone concerned about the conflict of interest? And see the cafeteria ladies? Their hair nets, the gloves? They say it's to keep our food sanitary— but what if it's to keep *them* safe from our food?"

"I only buy milk," the neon girl replied. "We can always trust cows." She was probably just being nice. Weird, but nice.

"I'm not hungry," I said.

The cafeteria seating was organized by class. After finding our homeroom's table, I spotted Hailey and waved wildly. She seemed startled but managed a weak little smile. For the first time all morning, the knot in my stomach loosened. My whole body relaxed. I walked around the table and sat down next to her.

"You're not eating?" she asked, avoiding eye contact.

"You know how first days are," I said in a con- fiding tone. When she scooted away, I did too, so that our legs were still touching. We were probably making room for more friends. She was thoughtful! I liked that about her. "I've been so excited to meet my new best friend that my appetite is gone."

"That's nice," she said politely, inching away again. Down at the other end of the table, two of my pod-mates were watching me. The big kid was gone, I realized. He must've slipped out of line in the hall when the teacher had turned away.

I scooted closer, closing the gap between us yet

again. Hailey was still smiling, although her eyebrows went up, so her expression looked more like panic. But not everyone has time to practice in front of a mirror like I do.

"So, tell me about yourself," I said. "Don't leave out anything personal."

Instead of acknowledging my efforts, she froze, an expression of fear creeping across her face.

"What's wrong?" I whispered, leaning over. "Do you see dead people?" I held for the laugh.

"What is your problem?" another girl snapped at me as she came up to our table with her lunch tray. I recognized her from our class: impeccably dressed, with smooth brown hair and deep blue eyes. "Hailey," she said, speaking to my best friend, "is this girl bothering you?"

I gave the girl my most dazzling smile. She looked blankly at me, not returning it. Were these people ignorant of the laws of science? What would fail next? Gravity?

"You want to sit?" I asked. She probably just wanted me to scoot over more and make room for her, so I did, bumping up against Hailey and gently pushing her down the row, extra-especially careful not to leave an inch of space between us. She seemed upset about something. I wanted to make sure she felt comforted.

"Why don't we all introduce ourselves?" I suggested. "I'm Lizbeth, obviously." I thumped the name tag on my chest.

"I'm Sydney," the brown-haired girl said, eyeing me with a strangely hostile expression. "I see you already met my best friend, Hailey."

"It's my first day," I said, ignoring her comment. I'd straighten out any confusion about best friendships with Hailey later. "I'm excited about making new friends."

"What about your pod-mates?" Sydney asked. A few girls quietly snickered.

I glanced down the table. The momma's boy didn't have any lunch in front of him, although I had seen him carrying a paper bag when he got out of his mom's car this morning. The neon girl was staring at her tray of food, not moving. The boy said something to her and she giggled uncontrollably until she snorted. He grabbed an orange off her plate and threw a bit of peel at her. They looked like they were having fun.

"Oh, I'm not friends with them," I said. "I just got assigned to them."

"Exactly." Sydney turned to face me. "The polite thing to do would be to sit with them." She paused and looked around the table at the other girls as if looking for support. No one held her gaze or said anything back. "You probably don't know this, but most of us have been together since kindergarten. Most of us have played soccer on the same team since third grade. There's a reason we sit by ourselves. But I'm not trying to be mean."

"I'm sure you're not trying at all," I said, acting shocked at the suggestion.

A thin smile crept across her face. She got my sense of humor? The girl who disliked me for no reason was the only one who knew how funny I was!

"So you understand." Sydney continued to smile, but her eyes were cold. "You know, their pod was the only one with an empty seat. They needed a new friend. No one else did."

I didn't want a group of friends forced onto me. I wanted to force my friendship on someone else. Why did life take away all my choices?

The girls looked at me, their faces blank. Except for Sydney. She was beaming like a saint. I wanted to staple a halo onto her head. If my cosplay stuff wasn't in storage, I could have, too.

"But I promise we're not being mean, okay?" she said, as if she was worried about me. Her sweet manner left something to be desired. Like a soul.

"May I be excused?" I blurted out, my body going numb. The girls stifled giggles as Sydney's eyes danced. I had said the wrong thing, again. I tend to talk without thinking when I'm upset. I had planned on getting laughs today, but not on getting laughed at.

I stood and walked toward the door, trying to steady myself. My stomach cramped as a wave of homesickness hit me. Sydney was lucky. Like her, I used to go to school with kids I'd grown up with. I knew how safe and comfortable that was.

Being alone at school hurt like a giant-sized invisible pinch.

The restrooms were outside on the right . . . very, very close to the cafeteria. Someone knew more about the food here than I did.

Grateful for the privacy, I opened the stall door and sat down. It was refreshing to sit on a toilet without getting a head injury. I gently touched the back of my head and found a lump the size of an avocado pit. The edges were tender, making me wince when I prodded too hard.

Studies show that toxins are released from the body in our tears. I let a few tears fall, purely for scientific reasons. I'm good at crying, by the way. I can do the anime waif with a single tear rolling down one cheek. Or shoulder-shaking sobs. At the moment, I was somewhere in the middle. Reaching around with one hand, I tried patting myself in a comforting way, like a parent might do.

Without warning, the toilet flushed automatically, splashing water on the back of my pants. Too late, I leaped to my feet. I had a giant wet stain across my rear end, as if I had peed myself.

Once again, betrayed by indoor plumbing.

I threw open the door to the stall, looking around for a solution. Instead of paper towels, the restroom had a hot air hand dryer. I smacked the button, turned around, and bent over. With any luck, my pants would be dry before the lunch hour ended. No one would even notice my temporary absence.

Moments later, though, Ms. Farris' voice cut through the low roar of the dryer. She had obviously retrieved the class from the cafeteria and stopped them just outside the door.

"If anyone needs to use the restroom, you may do so now," Ms. Farris said.

Hailey threw open the door and froze, mouth gaping, staring at the new kid bent over with hot air blowing on her big wet butt.

I managed to lift one hand in a weak hello.

Ms. Farris acted quickly, pulling the door shut, but not before Hailey scrambled to avoid being trapped in the restroom with me. Out in the hall, I heard giggles turn into howls of laughter. Ms. Farris snapped commands to be quiet and keep moving.

The longest walk of my life was from that restroom to Room 223. This day had been an absolute disaster. What really hurt was that any of these events, if they had happened at my old school with my old friends, would have been hilarious to me.

As I entered the classroom, everyone was whispering and giggling, but not the good kind of giggling. Ms. Farris coughed into a tissue but it sounded like even she was stifling a laugh.

Why did people who didn't even know me want to make fun of me? And why had Sydney immediately cast me as the villain? The worst part was that she was the only one so far who understood how funny I actually was.

She murmured to a boy named Nick at her table, and as soon as Ms. Farris' back was turned, he lobbed a spitball at me. It splattered against my sleeve.

Spit is my Kryptonite. I froze, staring at the glistening mark on my sleeve. Biting my lower lip to keep my chin from trembling, I focused on breathing.

The neon girl across from me stood up, glaring at all the kids in the classroom. "May I get a tissue?"

Ms. Farris muttered yes, not paying any attention as she flipped through her lesson planner. When my pod-mate passed Sydney's table, she swiveled her head and practically hissed at them. "Leave her alone, you jerks."

My heart warmed just a bit.

"Or what, Tess? Is your magic chicken gonna get me?" Nick sneered.

So her name was Tess. And she had a magic chicken. I really wanted to go home.

Tess leaned toward him and he backed away. "What makes you think I'll wait for the chicken?"

A guy at the next pod, who had buzz-cut hair and cold eyes, jabbed a finger in the direction of the smaller guy in our pod. "Don't make life more difficult for your little friend, Tess."

"Tommy, if you didn't have an older brother—"

"But I do."

Ms. Farris clapped her hands together and Tess returned to our pod, red in the face and scowling. She handed the tissue to me without a glance or a word.

With all the plans I had made, I hadn't planned on walking right into a drama already in progress. But Tess had stood up for me, and I hadn't really done anything to deserve it. I tried to smile at her but my mouth wasn't working well. It still wanted to frown.

"Thank you, Tess." I turned to my other pod-mates. "What are your names?"

"Joseph," murmured the smaller guy.

The big guy next to me leaned over. "I am Groot." His eyes sparkled as if he wanted me to laugh with him, or even at him, but he definitively wasn't making fun of me.

Tess burst out laughing but quickly put her head on the desk to avoid detection. Ms. Farris looked up from her desk and frowned at me. At me!

Ms. Farris lifted her index finger. "You are at One, Lizbeth. Do not let me get to Three."

"How did I get to One?" I asked, confused.

Ms. Farris went back to writing at her desk, ignoring my question. Perhaps she assumed it was rhetorical.

"Excuse me, Ms. Farris, allow me to recap for clarity, if I may. I am at One, and my assignment is to stop you from getting to Three." I pulled out a notebook and pen.

Ms. Farris audibly exhaled.

"Is there a code word we can use?" I asked. "If you feel yourself moving toward Three, shout the code word. I'll stop whatever I'm doing and come running. You will never get to Three. Not on my watch, ma'am." I sat very straight, lifting my chin.

Some of my classmates were snickering. Again.

Ms. Farris pulled a slip of paper out of her desk and held it out to me.

DISCIPLINE SLIP

Please review with your child's behavior with them today. Please prepare your child to make better choices tomorrow.

PARENTAL SIGNATURE HERE:

I glanced down at my stupid name tag, thinking about everything that should have been written on it.

I placed my backpack on my desk and rested my head on it, facedown. When I inhaled, the mesh on the front pocket was sucked into my nostril. The raspy noise my breath made was so reassuring. Finally, I had found one natural law that actually worked in this strange place. In and out, I listened to the sound of reliability.

The bell rang and I lifted my head. My classmates were staring at me, wide-eyed, like I was the confusing one. Hailey refused to even make eye contact.

Joseph leaned across the table. "What doesn't kill you makes you stranger. Right?"

My mouth fell open. Then I giggled and he grinned at me, maybe relieved that I got the joke. Groot and Tess exchanged glances, and something seemed to be decided for them.

The first thing Joseph ever said to me, and he quoted the Joker?

Maybe this pod wasn't all bad. Maybe they were cool people disguised as weirdos, kind of like me.

CHAPTER 4

"Oh." Mom cleared her throat as we pulled into the driveway of our temporary house. "I didn't realize he was coming over."

Dad got out of his car with a big stuffed animal, a dog with long floppy ears. Camden and Eva had encouraged me to donate all my stuffed animals before the move. I was too old for stuffed animals now, according to them. But suddenly, I was glad my friends weren't here to see my excitement.

"With presents?" Mom sounded perplexed. Then her eyes narrowed.

That's when I saw Claire sitting in the passenger seat of Dad's car. She looked surprisingly human in daylight. But she had never been to our new place. I refused to let her so much as set foot on our driveway.

I jumped out of the car and ran for the front door.

"Agh!" I yelled. "No one move! I'll get the glue traps!"

"Come back, peaches!" Dad said as I dashed past him.

"Where are you going?" Mom called. "I don't see a rat." I glanced back at her. She threw one hand over her mouth as her eyes crinkled up. I wanted to kiss her! She got my joke!

Except it was no joke.

One time at a comics convention panel I went to with Dad, an actor said that he accidently got sick filming a scene because he didn't know that the set designer had used shaving cream instead of whipped cream for the milkshakes. Shaving cream stays fluffy under the hot set lights. Claire was like that: she looked pretty but I felt sick after being around her. She needed to change her name to Eek-Claire, like a polluted pastry. If Dracula's castle had a coffee shop, she'd be on the menu.

"Then I'll get some garlic. Her kind is repelled by it."

Mom turned toward Dad, palms raised, as if to say she had no part in this.

Mom had hidden a spare key under the planter next to the front door, so I fished it out and let myself inside.

The garlic was on the kitchen counter with a bag of onions. I didn't have pockets in my pants, or a fast way to string the garlic into a necklace, so I yanked my bralette open and stuffed the garlic inside. Just to be safe, I threw a couple of onions in as well before running back out.

"The sun will be setting soon!" I yelled. "Her power will have no limits!"

I pulled on Mom and Dad's hands, trying to drag them to safety, but neither moved. Claire remained in Dad's car, looking infuriatingly unthreatened by this turn of events.

"Peaches," Dad said, "I wanted to give you a present, okay? I didn't mean to upset you."

"Sweetheart." Mom joined in too, as if I was behaving irrationally. I wasn't the one who had split up a perfectly good family. "How about you just say 'thank you' and go inside?" She looked at Dad. "And the next time you decide to change our arrangements, you need to give me advance warning."

"Warning? I'm her dad." Dad disentangled himself from my grip, leaving me holding the stuffed dog. "I just thought a goofy present after her first day of school would make her happy. Is there something wrong with being happy?"

"I thought we weren't going to fight over this."

Dad took a long, meditative breath before answering. "It's been two years. I've done a lot of thinking. It's not enough to just stop by now and then."

Those were the exact words I had wished he would say to her someday, but the delivery was all wrong. Also, he was not holding a bouquet of roses. I glanced at Mom. Her face was pale.

He got back in the car and pulled out of the driveway. The streets in this neighborhood were old and narrow, though. He'd have to drive all the way to the end of the cul-de-sac down the street before he could turn around and leave for real.

I held up the stuffed dog for inspection. It looked real. There was a card on its collar, which Mom grabbed.

"Why did Dad give me this?" I decided to call him Potatoes. The name just came to me.

"It's from both of them." She held the card out. "They hope you love it. They say it will be cute on the bed Dad bought you for his apartment."

Dad drove past slowly. I saw him behind the wheel, watching my reaction to his—their—gift.

I dropkicked Potatoes across the driveway, making him bounce off the trashcan. With a half-strangled battle cry, I ran to retrieve him, held his fluffy butt right to my foot, and then let loose another vicious kick. Potatoes flew through the air, landing on Dad's windshield. Dad hit the brakes, swerving. Potatoes rolled off the hood and Dad accidently ran him over. Claire's mouth fell open in shock.

Dad stopped the car. But another car had just rolled around the corner and was bearing down on him fast. The other driver honked, urging Dad forward. There was no room for him to pull over, so he was forced to keep going. My eyes met Claire's as my victory sank in. She hadn't set one foot onto our temporary property and she never would.

After bowing with one hand at my waist, I walked inside without a second glance back.

Sighing, I collapsed on the couch, yanked the nametag off my shirt, and stuck the edge of it to a corner of the coffee table. I had always thought getting a "fresh start" meant a do-over, but that's not true. It's just a new zip code slapped on your old problems.

Mom opened the freezer. "Pizza?" she asked. "Pepperoni or cheese?"

I threw one hand over my forehead. "What I want doesn't come in a cardboard box!"

I cracked one eye open. She was waiting.

"Pepperoni." Skipping lunch had left me extremely hungry.

Before she hit the button to start the oven, she looked at me sternly. "But we need to talk about what happened tonight, okay? Maybe not now, but soon. I don't like to see you so angry."

I swallowed. "Do I have to live with Dad? Is that why he bought me that stuffed animal? And mentioned a bed for me in his apartment?"

"No." Her face softened. Sometimes when I asked hard questions, she got soft and quiet. That helped us both to think. "I'm sure he just meant he wants to see you more. Which is good news. Really."

"Okay." My stomach began to settle. For a moment, I had thought I was going to have to leave Mom and face Claire on a regular basis.

Mom wrinkled her nose. "And take the garlic out of your bra."

The next morning, I was holding the classroom door open, smiling brightly as I spied Hailey coming down the hallway. Sydney was with her but I didn't let that bother me. I was going to be best friends with Hailey whether she liked me or not.

"Good morning!" I chirped.

They glided in past me, so close I could tell you what laundry softener their families used. Neither spoke to me or made eye contact. They pretended they didn't see me. No wonder schools do vision tests.

Tess and Joseph rounded the corner next, with Groot right behind them. Tess waved at me, and the guys jerked their chins up and to the left, which I think is how middle-school guys signal recognition. Tess's shirt had a picture of flying kittens in space, with the planets embellished in a yellow so bright it hurt my eyes.

As they approached, I realized how big Groot really was. Not just tall; he was wide, too, and muscular. I was trying not to stare when Tess grabbed my arm.

"Sit with us at lunch today, okay?"

"We have to introduce you to SuperChicken," Joseph added.

"Not on her second day." Groot shook his head. He nudged them toward the door and I stepped aside to let them through.

Alone in the hall, I peered into the classroom. Yesterday had been disastrous. Today my plan was to not have a plan, which meant everything was guaranteed to be better. That was pure logic.

While I was thinking through my non-plan, the tardy bell rang. Too late, I scooted through the door.

Ms. Farris glanced up from her computer. "Well, look who has joined us."

Heads swiveled as if they were on sticks, those vacant eyes feasting on me. It was like a scene out of a zombie movie.

"Welcome back," she began, then hesitated. "Um . . . Elizabeth."

"It's Lizbeth, actually," I said, my hands clenched tight at my sides. I did not want another bad day here.

"So today it's Lizbeth-Actually," Ms. Farris replied, and held for a beat, but I didn't laugh, if that's what she was waiting for. Being tardy had disoriented me. I'd never been tardy. What came next?

Her eyes narrowed as she pointed to my shirt. I looked down.

"Looks like you forgot something, too," she said.

I'd left my name tag at home!

A horrible feeling, like a spider dropping from the ceiling onto my shoulder, fell over me. And I accidently blurted out a word that should only be used when discussing what beavers build. The class erupted in howls of laughter.

With one hand, Ms. Farris beckoned me forward. She opened her desk drawer and handed me a slip of paper.

THIS IS YOUR SECOND
DISCIPLINE SLIP

Please review your child's behavior with them today. Please prepare your child to make better choices tomorrow. Failure to return this slip by the next school day will result in detention.

PARENTAL SIGNATURE HERE:

The American justice system rests on the principle that adults are innocent until proven guilty. Justice in public school says kids are guilty, until proven guiltier. But see, I hadn't meant to use that word. I'd never, ever used it in school before. I was a first-time offender. Again.

Ms. Farris scribbled something and then handed me a fresh name tag. "I suggest you do not lose that one."

HELLO
MY NAME IS
Lizbeth

"I won't." I made my way back to my pod, keeping my eyes down. There was a hungry energy buzzing in the room. These strangers relished my humiliation. Why? I hadn't done anything to them.

Tommy watched me as I walked past. "Maybe you should write *Forgetful* on it," he said just loudly enough for me to hear.

"Is that one of the Seven Dwarves?" a girl named Lucy asked, looking confused. I glanced at Hailey, hoping she'd stick up for me.

"I think we'll just call you LivesWet," Sydney said.

Oof. Sydney got the huge laugh from the class that I had been hoping for since my arrival. Hailey laughed harder than anyone.

I stood at the front of the lunch line in disbelief. "Wait," I said. "That's it?"

The cashier murmured a yes, waving for me to move on.

Going through the lunch line had been unavoidable today, so I had chosen the food least likely to kill me or deforest the planet, then held my breath as I "paid." The cashier lady punched a button on her computer screen. *That's it.*

"Hold on. You hit one button and I get all this food? Even the cheese?" I had grabbed cheese strings in a plastic package. They looked pricey but they were small enough that I didn't think I'd need my lactase pills.

"Yes, honey."

"I need you to double check," I said quietly.

A teacher on lunch duty approached. "What's the problem here?"

"No problem. Just a new student." The cashier waved her away, and then lowered her head to be closer to me. "What's up?"

Cupping my hands, I whispered in her ear. "My mom's broke. She can't pay for all this. I thought maybe you were supposed to take something off my plate when no one was looking."

She pulled back, winking at me. "Nope. You're all set. This school has its issues, but we've at least got that figured out." She glanced over at my class table. "Besides, you have enough to worry about."

I smiled back without even trying and glanced at the gold-colored name tag she wore. "Thank you, Ms. Tyler."

"See you tomorrow, Lizbeth."

Surprised, I remembered I was wearing a name tag, too, then grinned. It was refreshing to hear myself called by my real name, instead of LivesWet.

As I walked to the table, Hailey looked away. I knew she'd seen me. Of course, it's a well-established fact that mean girls ignore you to hurt your feelings. But why would she want to hurt my feelings? We didn't even know each other. And I was awesome.

On the other hand, nice people pretend they don't see you, too, but only because they *don't* want to hurt your feelings. Maybe this was all a big misunderstanding. Maybe the real problem here was Sydney.

I set my tray next to Joseph, across from Tess. On the way to lunch, Groot had sneaked away down a quiet hallway, so it was just us. Joseph stared at my tray a moment or two longer than would be considered polite. He didn't have any food.

"Where's your lunch?" I asked. "You came in with a lunch bag today."

He turned red and looked away.

"That lady will feed you for free. Even cheese!" I informed him. "Tell her Lizbeth sent you." A light went on in the dim recesses of my brain: the genesis of a new plan for getting rid of Claire.

He scowled, hunched over the table. "It's not about money."

I pushed my tray toward him, distracted by this feeling that I was about to have a great idea. "You want my orange? At least, I think it's an orange. It's somewhat pale. It might be a dying grapefruit."

Tess grabbed it. She sank her two front teeth into it, then jammed a finger into the cut and began peeling it. She stuck her nose into the gap and sniffed.

"It's an orange, all right," she announced. "Would you like me to peel it the rest of the way?"

"Do you . . . want it?" I asked weakly. I felt like I had just witnessed a crime.

"Gross, no. I hate oranges." She rolled it across the table to me. Joseph intercepted it and took a bite, spitting a piece of peel at Tess. She batted it away with one hand, not paying any attention, as if this was normal behavior.

"Joseph, you better eat that," Tommy called

from down at the end of the table. "You need your strength."

Joseph ducked his head, his cheeks turning red. I didn't know if it was anger, embarrassment, or both. Two days in a row, I'd seen him come to school with a lunch. Both days, he'd sat at our table empty-handed. What happened to his lunch in between the carpool lane and the cafeteria? I didn't think Joseph would want me to ask, so I didn't. But I wondered if it had anything to do with Groot.

"So," I said, turning to Tess. "You wanted to explain about this chicken?"

"SuperChicken," Tess said, her voice extra loud.

"Keep your voices down." Joseph glanced from side to side.

I followed his gaze and noticed some older boys at another table watching Joseph, their eyes narrow and mean. They nudged each other, smirking and gesturing toward him.

At our table, Tommy turned to the older boys and nodded. I figured his older brother, the one Tess had mentioned, was one of them.

"Can you come over to my house tomorrow?" Tess asked me. "We can hang out and we'll have privacy to discuss all things SuperChicken."

I bit my lip to hold in a snarky response. Then all at once, a plan came together in my brain. "Where do you live?"

When she told me, I realized it was just far enough away from my temporary house that my next attempt to rid my family of Claire might actually work.

"Do you have a printer?" I asked. She didn't get a chance to answer.

"Good afternoon, students!" Ms. Camp, the principal, waltzed to the front of the cafeteria, interrupting our conversation. I made a mental note to explain my plan to Tess later.

"I've got a quick announcement to make," Ms. Camp began. "For months now, adults have been fighting behind closed doors about the future of this school's arts programming, which is in danger of being discontinued due to lack of funding. I know you all love your art and music classes and your access to our wonderful media center, and it would be a tragedy to lose these cornerstones of your educational experience. The issues are complicated, but they don't have to be."

Was anyone even listening? I turned around to scan the crowd. Joseph poked me in the ribs, frowning. "Don't let them catch you looking."

"If our community and our school board see something special here," Ms. Camp continued, "we can win this fight. A wise man named Socrates once said, 'Wisdom begins with wonder.' Let's show the community how a strong arts program creates wise and wonder-filled students."

She gestured dramatically toward a man who was leaning against the cafeteria doors. He wore a jean jacket and splattered khaki pants rolled at the ankles. He was old but not ancient, maybe in his twenties, and he had penetrating eyes that swept the room, studying us like we were zoo exhibits.

Ms. Camp beamed at him. "You all know our art teacher, Mr. Westchester. He has agreed to help organize this year's talent show. Our music teacher, Ms. Mayweather, will be assisting."

A chorus of groans was the only evidence that Ms. Mayweather held a job here.

"This annual event is a beloved Plains Creek Middle School tradition, and this year we're going to take it to the next level. So . . ."

Ms. Camp paused for a moment as if waiting for her own imaginary drumroll.

". . . every one of you will be participating this year."

Students exchanged terrified glances. Talent shows are the definition of middle school horror. Worse than Scoliosis Check day. Worse than changing in the locker room for PE. Even I, a consummate performer, hate talent shows on principle. Cosplay costumes? Not a category I could enter. Special effects makeup? Also not a category. Anything I might one day win an Oscar for is not included in talent shows.

"The talent show will take place in the gymnasium the last Friday of the quarter, just over three weeks from now, and it will be open to the public. Admission will be pay-what-you-can, and all the donations will go toward our art and music classes. We've invited five school board members to act as judges, and the winner will receive a certificate!"

Since we'd just come from the gym, I knew there was a curtained stage at one end of it, presumably for school-wide events like the nightmare Ms. Camp was describing.

"You have until next Monday to decide on your act or project, and to choose partners if you want to perform in a group," Ms. Camp went on. "Your homeroom teacher will be passing around a sign-up sheet. To recap, participation is mandatory, and every entry must reflect how the arts program enriches your education."

The older boys at the other table called Joseph's name softly. "Joooseph. Hey, Jooooooseph. We'll plan your act."

Tommy looked down the table at Joseph. "If you even try to enter some stupid picture of your stupid chicken, I'll smash your face in. My brother wants you to do a talent act."

I sneaked another look at them and saw the only guy in school who was nearly as big as Groot. He had a face like a doorstop. His expression said he was the kind of guy who actually enjoyed stopping doors with his face. That had to be Tommy's brother.

I shuddered, turning back around. No wonder Tommy got away with bullying other kids.

"I think I'm going to vomit," Joseph moaned. Tess reached across the table for his hand but he pulled away.

"Get Paul," Tess urged me.

I stared at her blankly. I had never heard of Paul.

"Groot!" she said. "Go find Groot!"

CHAPTER 5

Groot shuffled across the hall, from one classroom to another. Ducking into a doorway, I leaned out to watch. What was he up to?

I heard a low voice, deep and rich, begin singing a slow song in a language I didn't know. This wasn't the kind of music that I normally listened to on my phone or that Mom played on the radio. This was invisible medicine, taking me by surprise, comforting me. I rested my head against the doorway, eyes closed. Anyone who said there was no such thing as magic had never heard this voice.

"Uh, what are you doing?"

I opened my eyes. Groot stood in front of me, scowling. The music had stopped.

"You interrupted the singing!" I said.

Groot frowned, looking around, then raised his

eyebrows. "Oh, yeah. That's the janitor."

"What are *you* doing over here?" I demanded, feeling suddenly suspicious of him.

"I feed all the class animals during lunch."

I narrowed my eyes at him. "Did you steal Joseph's lunch?"

"What? No." His expression turned dark, anger lighting his eyes.

I stepped back. "Sorry, Groot. It's just that Joseph has his lunch in the morning, but then at lunch time he doesn't, and you sneak off by yourself around the same time."

"My name is Paul." He folded his massive arms, glaring at me. "I was trying to make you laugh when I said my name was Groot. You looked miserable."

"I like Groot better," I replied.

"Get over it."

Whoa. He really liked his name, I guess.

"Oh!" My brain suddenly began working again. "Tess wanted me to come find you. Ms. Camp declared that the whole school has to participate in a talent show and the older boys are trying to force Joseph to do something embarrassing. Plus, he doesn't have his lunch again today. If you're not taking it, I bet those boys are. We should rough them up."

"Rough them up? How much TV do you watch?"

"It depends. I used to watch a lot of anime with my dad, but lately our interests have diverged."

Paul shook his head, then turned and walked in the direction of the cafeteria. "You don't like bullies, do you?"

"No one likes bullies."

"Their moms do. Their moms probably think they're wonderful. Parents never have a clue. And the school administration is just as useless. They have no idea what goes on here." He ran a hand through his hair as he walked, looking stressed. "But I'm three times your size and you confronted me about Joseph's lunch? You've got courage. That's cool."

"But what about the talent show?" I asked. We were almost back to the cafeteria. "And those bullies? What are you going to do?"

"I can pound any of those guys into dust and they all know it. As long as I'm standing next to Joseph, they don't bother him."

"You can't stand next to him forever." I instinctively grabbed his arm. "You need a plan."

He removed my hand, and his hands were surprisingly soft. My cheeks got hot and prickly and my stomach fluttered. Whether it was fear from daring to grab a giant or something much worse, like hormones, I didn't know. But I definitely felt something. Something scary and uncomfortable.

"Nah, we don't need a plan. We have each other. And now you." He held my gaze, then smiled finally. "Welcome to the resistance."

Joseph seemed to calm down once I brought Paul back within a five-foot radius of him. Meanwhile, the whole school was in an uproar about the talent show. People were already sorting themselves into groups, mostly by pod. Tess explained that pods were generally determined based on two factors: on-level or advanced classes, and whose parents wrote notes insisting on seat assignment. The talent show would be class warfare with a curtain and applause. "What are we going to do?" Joseph asked, hunched over, whispering.

Groot—I mean, Paul—looked around, then focused on me. "Got any talents we should know about?"

"I cosplay—or I used to, with my dad," I said.

Joseph lit up. "That's so cool! I've always wanted to do that!"

"Everything is in storage, though, even my mom's sewing machine." I felt helpless.

"We can decide on a project later," Tess said breezily. "For now, are we agreed that the four of us will be a team?"

"This is so unfair!" Joseph protested. "We're all going to be forced to stand on stage and perform in front of the kids who make fun of us."

"The talent show isn't really about talent," Tess reminded him. "It's about saving the arts program."

"Or it would be," said Paul, "if that plan was actually going to work. Ms. Camp can't seriously think a handful of donations will make that much of a difference."

An unsettled, heavy feeling blanketed us. Each of us sat in silence for a minute, pinned under the weight of our own worries.

"So, we're hanging out after school tomorrow, right?" Tess piped up eventually, looking at me.

"If you have a printer, then yes."

"We do, but why do you need a printer?"

"My dad is dating a human cockroach and I need to get rid of her," I replied. My new plan bordered on evil genius, but I couldn't decide which way it tilted.

"But I need to initiate you into the mysteries of SuperChicken." She folded her arms.

I raised my eyebrows. "Sounds like a busy afternoon."

Finally, she nodded. "I will prepare snacks."

Being around Tess was wonderfully strange. How could a new friend already feel like an old friend?

Raindrops raced down the kitchen windows. Mom was making soup for dinner while I sat at the table with her laptop. I closed the browser tab with a sigh. Camden and Eva had posted pictures of themselves studying at Eva's house. The pillowcase we'd all signed in Sharpie was in the background of one photo. I never thought I'd be the person missing from that photo, or that life. I hadn't even moved that far away, but I'd barely heard from them lately.

Following them online made me feel so alone. I posted three hearts and three happy-face emojis anyway. Secretly I hoped they remembered that there used to be three of everything, including us.

Thunder rumbled from far away. I wished it

would come closer. I'd always loved storms—the drama of wind and lightning, how everything bends and blows and dances. Tonight, I needed to be around an old friend, someone who knew me. Thunder was that friend.

While I waited for the storm to move in, I wasted a few more minutes online, diagnosing myself with rare diseases. With every click, I was led into increasingly less reliable territory.

"For $29.99, a guy is offering a do-it-yourself exorcism kit guaranteed to remove any kind of supernatural manifestation," I told Mom.

"Something on your mind?" she replied as she stirred the soup.

"It's not for me, obviously. But one of my pod-mates at school is having an issue with bullies. And there's a talent show coming up. Maybe I could perform an exorcism on a bully for the talent show."

"Bullies are a completely natural phenomenon, unfortunately," she said. "And you are not responsible for fixing their behavior." She stopped and turned to face me, with one hip leaned against the stove. "Just focus on what you can actually change, okay? Any energy spent trying to change another person is wasted energy."

She returned to stirring the soup, sighing. She looked fragile, like one more piece of bad news would crush her.

Finding out that her daughter had gotten in trouble at school for the first time seemed to qualify as bad news. Which was why I decided to spare her this distressing knowledge.

A few short keystrokes later, I was working on my new plan. I jotted down some helpful notes.

- No one signs their name the same way every time.
- Do not trace. Tracing a signature will always look fake.
- Find a letter or loop that makes the signature unique. Focus on copying that.

FBI handwriting analysis experts don't earn as much as special effects artists, but they have better dental care plans.

Now, here is an example of my mother's signature, as seen in her checkbook, which was conveniently in her laptop bag.

Margaret Murphy

Pausing, I reminded myself that I had to protect her from more stress. So this was important.

This was my first attempt at her signature:

Margaret Murphy

I gasped. The Universe had entrusted me with yet another gift.

"What are you working on?" Mom was still stirring, with a faraway look, as if heating up soup was a form of meditation.

"I'm practicing cursive." This was true. "Schools don't teach cursive anymore, you know."

She smiled! "I love that about you." She turned off the heat on the stove and got out two bowls. "You're always exploring new challenges."

My heart did a little dance as I folded the paper and stuffed it in my pocket. I closed the browser window and moved the computer to the other end of the table, where Dad was supposed to sit.

"Of those to whom much is given, much is required." President John F. Kennedy said that once in a famous speech, although he was copying Jesus. Both men are still very well-regarded in certain circles. I was thinking about that in my room after dinner as I executed my plan. The forgery took under thirty seconds, and I decided to recycle the practice paper tomorrow at school. Everyone won, even the environment. Triumphantly, I tucked both pages into my backpack. All I needed was a cape and I'd be a sixth-grade superhero.

The next morning, after Mom dropped me off, I decided to wait for the first bell inside the girls' restroom. Paul had assumed I wanted to be part of the "resistance," but I didn't know exactly what or who we were resisting. Or what was required of me as a resistor. Until I understood what was going on, I probably shouldn't get involved. I didn't want to get into any actual trouble.

I swung the door open, startling Hailey. She was perched on the edge of a sink with a missing faucet, looking at her phone. Glancing under the stalls, I realized we were alone.

"Where's Sydney?" I asked.

"Her grandma died again," Hailey muttered.

"Again?"

"Long story," Hailey said, swiping the image on her screen. "She'll come back next week, I think."

"The grandma?"

Hailey looked up, frowning. "No. Sydney."

Sydney was going to be gone for the rest of the week? This sounded promising.

"Maybe we can start over," I said, taking a deep breath. "Get to know each other. I'm sure you think I am weird. I'm not. I actually identify as quirky."

Instead of laughing, she just nodded, still staring at her screen.

"First impressions can be wrong," I continued, my voice a higher pitch than normal. Coughing, I continued. "For example, I might've assumed you were dumb. Sidekicks usually are. But you're not."

Hailey looked up, glaring. "I'm not the sidekick."

"Well, so . . . if I'm not the weird girl and you're not the dumb sidekick," I said, "maybe we can be friends?"

Hailey hopped down from the sink and tucked her phone in the back pocket of her jeans. I racked my brain for a way to keep the conversation going.

"Why are you hiding in here?" I asked. She didn't answer so I tried to soften the question. "It doesn't make sense. You've got a million friends."

"Because Sydney isn't here. Ms. Farris is going to have us pick partners for the science project that's due next Wednesday, and Sydney was supposed to be mine. Now I'm going to get assigned to someone that no one else wanted either."

I gasped in delight. "Hey, I don't have a partner!"

Her lips curled into a thin smile.

I cleared my throat. "I see your point."

"So, I'll ask you a question," she said. "Why do you want to be friends with me? We don't have anything in common. We aren't the kind of people who normally hang out together."

"You looked like someone I was friends with. At my old school."

"You miss her?"

"I miss . . . everything." Sitting at the dinner table with Mom and Dad, giggling in a blanket fort with Camden and Eva, walking up and down the aisles at fabric stores with Mom while Dad bought foam and glue for costumes. My whole world had been make-believe, only I had never known it.

The bell rang and Hailey headed for the door. She held it open and I realized she was waiting for me. As fast as I could, I followed her, feeling really grateful and confused.

As soon as the morning announcements were over, Ms. Farris began roll call. When she got to my name, I reached into my backpack and grabbed the discipline slip. My conscience chose this moment to turn against me.

Last night, I had been confident that forging Mom's signature was best for everyone. But now my brain was screaming that this was wrong.

It was too late to lose my nerve now. Springing to my feet, I hustled to her desk and thrust the paper at her before she even asked me for it.

I held out the slip with a stiff arm, unwilling to look at it. Ms. Farris barely glanced up as she grabbed it and tossed it onto the growing pile of papers on her desk.

Mission accomplished. My cheeks were hot, but I figured that was because the whole plan had gone amazingly well.

My next plan went into motion during science class. "Partners, one of you needs to write your names on the board," Ms. Farris said. "The other one can come up to my desk and draw a slip of paper from this bowl. The slip has your assigned topic for your Wednesday presentation."

Hailey approached the board and wrote her name. Then mine. She had to glance back at me and squint at my name tag to confirm the spelling.

The other girls in Hailey's clique stared at her. I struggled to read their expressions because horror, confusion, and despair all use the same facial muscles. However, I suspected that tales of this day would be handed down from generation to generation, how Great-Great-Grandma Hailey once had a normal life but then LivesWet ruined everything. My people would pass her people on the street and there would be insults.

It soon became clear that only one other person didn't have a partner: Groot. I mean, Paul. Once you've decided what someone is called, it's hard to change the name in your mind.

I glanced down at my lap, too embarrassed to look at my pod-mate. I hadn't known he needed a partner.

Mrs. Farris looked at Paul. "You can do this alone. You'll get extra credit, as usual."

Paul acknowledged this with a nod, not looking at her or me or anyone else. I felt like a jerk.

Students were drawing their topics from the bowl on Ms. Farris's desk. Glad to get up from my table, I zeroed in on the bowl and pulled out a slip of paper with one word. SUPERNOVA.

"We got a supernova!" I exclaimed. "That's way better than a regular nova!"

If this wasn't a thumbs-up from the Universe, I didn't know what was.

I couldn't wait to sit with Hailey at lunch. We got our trays and walked toward the class table together. She paused suddenly, eyeing Joseph and Tess. As usual, Paul was gone and Joseph didn't have anything to eat. Tess slipped him a cookie from her lunch bag. Joseph tilted his head back and balanced the cookie on his nose, and Tess immediately copied him.

"Tess and Joseph seem like good friends." Hailey had a faraway look in her eyes.

Tess and Joseph snapped their heads forward suddenly, their mouths open. Joseph caught his cookie and ate it. Tess's landed on the table and broke.

I wanted to hear what Joseph was saying, because Tess was giggling uncontrollably. Hailey's friends were whispering to each other as they watched, scowling.

"Yeah, they look out for each other," I said, then refocused on Hailey. "Wait—are you saying you wish you had friends like that?"

Hailey flinched and then walked the last few paces to her usual spot. "I'm just saying it's nice. They laugh all the time."

I squeezed in between her and Lucy, my butt resting on the gap between the benches. It felt like a clothespin pinching my rear.

"Hey!" Lucy waved for everyone's attention. "We can't wear red shirts next Wednesday. The football team is wearing their red jerseys to school for their game. They got rescheduled from Friday because the high schoolers need the field."

"Gross." This was the consensus. I didn't know if it applied to the boys or their jerseys.

Lucy continued. "So, Hailey decided that we should wear pink instead." Everyone agreed and went back to their little conversations. Hailey barely acknowledged them. I was surprised, though, that Hailey had made a decision for the whole group. She didn't seem like the take-charge type.

"So, Hailey," I said, retrieving my notes from my pocket, "let's talk supernovas."

She looked at me with an utterly blank expression, like her operating system had frozen. Her face was an Error Message.

"Our project? For class? We're doing supernovas." I felt ridiculous trying to bring her up to speed on her own assignment.

She blinked. Something had finally clicked inside her head. "Oh, I don't really care about that. I mean, I trust you completely."

She opened a little baggie of carrot sticks and leaned toward another girl, listening to her conversation. She trusted me completely. I decided this was a very positive sign.

A few minutes later, when we had finished eating, I tried again. "So, I'll just work on our report," I said, following Hailey to the trash cans to dump the empty cartons on our trays. "I already have, like, ten websites in mind to use as sources. For the class presentation, at first I thought we could make a big poster and draw a supernova and maybe diagram the full life cycle of a star. On the other hand, maybe it would be better to keep it simple. We could just play a video from NASA and then perform a monologue . . ."

Hailey cut me off. "We're only partners because Sydney is gone. Sydney does all this stuff for me. She doesn't pester me about the details, okay? Be like Sydney."

"I'm not sure that's possible. I was born, not spawned."

Hailey deposited her empty tray in the stack near the trash cans and headed back toward our table. "Listen. Sydney is under a lot of stress and unfortunately, her drama is affecting my grades. I need you to do a great job but I don't want to be involved."

"Stress? You mean her grandma?"

Hailey sighed. "Her grandma got taken to the hospital last month, and we all thought she was dead, but then she wasn't, so they brought her back home and started the countdown all over again. It was pretty intense."

"Sydney lives with her grandma?"

"Yeah, last year after her parents got divorced, she and her mom moved back in with her. Which, if you ask me, wasn't that smart because the grandma already had Alzheimer's. They were basically going from a bad situation to a worse one."

"She only moved here last year?" My mind was reeling. After all, Sydney was the one who'd made certain I knew how long the rest of the group had been together.

"Yeah. And she's been sad ever since she moved here. And I want to be supportive and whatever, but sometimes she's kind of high maintenance, and I have my own problems, right?"

We squeezed back into our spots at the table to wait out the rest of the lunch hour. Now I felt lousy that I'd labeled Sydney a cruel and cursed example of inhumanity. She was almost . . . relatable. Except for the fact that she had seemed determined to destroy me from the moment I arrived here.

"I need to stay focused on my grades," Hailey concluded, "because my parents want to transfer me to a school that has money and good teachers, unlike this one."

"So," I said slowly, thinking this through, "you want me to do all the work but you want to get an A. What's in it for me? When Sydney comes back, are you even going to talk to me?"

Hailey considered this. "If we get an A, you can be my friend. Sydney will just have to deal with it."

CHAPTER 6

The bus had the stale, heavy odor of livestock. Some kids had earbuds in; others stared straight ahead with dulled expressions. I'd never ridden a bus in this school district. The houses here were small and in need of paint. Cars with flat tires sat in cracked driveways. Back in my neighborhood, where my real house was, everything was bright and shiny. I liked bright and shiny. My throat got tight just thinking about how much I missed my old life.

"Haven't you ever ridden the bus before?" Tess asked. "You look a little sick."

"Just excited," I lied, focusing on why so many seats were torn and why "Jack Loves Kate." Or if he still did. "Hey, why is the emergency exit at the back of the bus?" I had turned to take in the complete panorama of vandalism when I spotted the sign. "If it's safer to get off back there, why wouldn't they want us to use that door all the time?"

"You sure talk a lot when you're freaking out," she said.

The bus lurched to a stop. Tess jumped up, grabbing my hand to pull me toward the appropriate exit.

Her street looked nearly identical to the one where I lived now. She had a tree in her front yard, too, and her tree didn't have any leaves left, either. I'd assumed that someone like Tess—someone so different—would live in a very different place.

A silent house greeted us when Tess unlocked the door and swung it open. Dust motes, caught by the light, swirled in the air. Her front room seemed a lot like the one in my temporary house: small, with a comfortable-looking old couch, plus a few photographs on a table by the door. The house had a faint smell of apples and cinnamon. Tess paused in the entryway, watching my reaction as I looked around.

"It's nice," I said.

She shrugged. "It's empty."

I could tell she wasn't talking about furniture. Houses feel weird when the parents aren't home, like the family is on pause. It isn't a bad feeling, just a sense that real life will happen later.

She dropped her backpack at the door and I followed her to the kitchen. On the counter sat the largest jar I'd ever seen, filled with the largest pickles I'd ever seen. They floated in a transparent green liquid, bunched together at the top, as if trying to escape.

She unscrewed the lid, stabbed a pickle with a fork and handed it to me, her eyes shining with unnerving delight. She speared one for herself next.

"You don't have to refrigerate dill pickles, did you know that?" Tess said, making a beeline for the laptop on the kitchen table. "They're fermented. That means an invisible chemical reaction turns a lowly cucumber into a glorious, tasty pickle."

"That's good. I guess."

"Good? It's great!" Tess exclaimed, setting her forked pickle aside. "Everyone hates cucumbers."

Opening the computer, she typed out a series of numbers and then jumped up again. After briefly dashing out of the room, she returned with a thick file folder. From this she withdrew a map of the world that she unfurled on the kitchen table. With a permanent marker, she began transferring the numbers to different points on the map. I decided silent observation was the best course for me to take for the time being.

She scratched her chin. "We'd better call Joseph."

A moment later Joseph's face appeared on the laptop screen. "What's up, Tess? Oh, hi, Lizbeth."

I waved.

"Joseph, have you seen all the activity near the Ring of Fire?"

"I just got home. I was playing a video game."

"This could be huge! The news channels are going to be interested in all sorts of theories. We could post about our theory that Earth is actually a giant egg, and the earthquakes mean SuperChicken is ready to hatch."

"No one is ever going to believe that," he said, rolling his eyes. "We made that up."

"That doesn't mean it doesn't deserve to get traction! It's free publicity, Joseph! And once we've stirred up a little attention, it'll be the perfect time to post the first SuperChicken graphic novel online!"

"Tess?" he asked.

She paused, waiting. My eyes darted back and forth between them.

"You're going to make us rich someday." Joseph ducked suddenly. "Gotta go. My mom's coming."

"Joseph is awesome," Tess said, as the call ended and she closed the program window, "but his mom treats him like a baby. I think it's because he's so small for his age." She finished her pickle, quietly nodding to herself as she munched. "I bet she'll get all of us out of the talent show, though. Joseph suggested our pod run the lights and music behind the scenes."

Shrugging, I took my first bite of pickle. "Oh!" It was amazing.

Tess's eyes cleared as she looked at me, nodding. "Right?"

"I always thought of pickles as the green things they hide under your burger buns. It made them seem a little sketchy."

"Pickles are underappreciated." Tess licked her fork, held it out to regard it, then gave me a sideways glance. "Pickles are the changelings of the vegetable world." I suspected she was testing me, to see if I even knew that word, *changeling*.

"Not really. A chemical reaction changes a cucumber into a pickle," I replied. "That's science, not science fiction."

Her eyes lit up before her face turned solemn. "Unless . . . they've secretly been pickles all along, waiting for the right moment to reveal their ultimate form." She lowered her voice to a whisper, glancing furtively from side to side. "They float among us."

When I cocked one eyebrow, she burst into giggles. Her eyes sparkled as she laughed.

"If pickles are sentient beings," I replied, "what does that make you? You just stabbed and ate that one."

Tess looked at her empty fork, then at the remaining pickles floating in the jar. "I'd like to revise my statement."

Now it was my turn to laugh. She was the weirdest girl I'd ever met, but maybe the funniest, too. Maybe I'd found bright and shiny after all. Isn't it possible that the Universe just keeps it in different places?

Clearing my throat, I pointed to the map on the table. "Explain."

"We will start at the beginning. One word: SuperChicken." She jabbed her fork in the air for emphasis, and I scooted back in my seat.

"A proper noun, a name, a title." Setting the fork back down, she took a notebook out of her file folder and flipped it open to reveal a sketch of a giant chicken standing next to a broken eggshell. The eggshell had different colors and shapes, and after a second I realized it was a globe. A broken globe. The chicken had hatched from an egg that looked like Earth.

"Welcome to SuperChicken 101. That's him, SuperChicken." She jabbed the paper with her finger. "Well, actually, probably Son of SuperChicken. We still don't know which came first, the chicken or the egg."

She paused, just as I would if I were holding for a laugh. I did a polite stage chuckle.

"Earth itself is a giant egg," she continued. "Scientists will tell you that Earth has lava at the center, but they lie! It's yolk. These earthquakes are the chicken growing, shifting inside his shell. One day he will emerge and only his faithful followers will be spared his wrath. On that day, you will have to know the sign of SuperChicken."

She extended the first three fingers on her right hand in the shape of a claw. "See? Only true believers know it. We use it to signal one another."

I practiced making the sign and she beamed with approval.

"SuperChicken will be pleased."

"But this is just a graphic novel, right?" I asked.

"It's much more than that." She grinned. "When Joseph and I were little, we made up these stories at recess every day. We worked on them so much that I think we even started to believe them. I mean, we knew a chicken wasn't going to save us, but we could pretend that the bullies would regret how they treated us. Dumb, I know. But stories are the only things that make people feel better."

"Not the only thing," I said. "Revenge is quite satisfying too. Which reminds me, I need to get to work."

While she helped me design a poster and print out eight copies—eight being the number of infinity, like my infinite loathing of Claire—she rambled on about her dreams for sharing SuperChicken with the world. Tess was a dreamer. I was a planner. Maybe we would make a good team.

We had just grabbed some thumbtacks and were about to venture out to post the signs on utility poles when we heard the sound of the garage door rumbling open.

"My dad!" Tess squealed.

Moments later, the door connecting the house to the garage opened. A guy burst in, clutching a cellphone to his ear and carrying a shoulder bag. Tess stood, arms extended for a hug. He held one finger to his lips, motioning for her to be quiet. She hadn't even said anything. When he saw me, he lowered the phone to his shoulder and whispered, "Good to see you again."

My right eyebrow shot up. He'd never seen me before.

Opening his laptop, he kept chatting nonstop about some project and its deadlines. Tess stared at her father. For a fraction of a second, I saw what I must look like when I stared at my dad.

I reached out and placed a hand on her shoulder. "I'm glad you're helping me with my problem. Maybe there's a way for me to help you with yours."

"He doesn't have a girlfriend I can get rid of." Tess looked down at the signs I was carrying. "Well, he won't mind if we go outside for a while . . ."

"Excellent. We have plenty of time till my mom picks me up." My plan was to cover as wide an area as possible in the window of opportunity we had.

This time, my plan had to work. Eliminating Claire would solve my problems and give me my old life back. That was my favorite kind of math. Take away one, get everything else added.

Tess was still studying the posters. "Are you sure this is a good idea?"

I flashed her the sign of SuperChicken. "Of all the ideas I've ever regretted, this is probably going to be my favorite."

"Can we hit Starbucks first?" I pleaded as Mom pulled into a parking space at the mall. Tess and I hadn't eaten anything besides pickles, and now I was exhausted from dashing around Tess's neighborhood. I doubted I could make it until dinner, much less my usual Friday night movie date with Mom, without some emergency caffeine and sugar.

"Let me see if I have any cash." After turning off the engine, Mom rummaged in her bag. Her phone buzzed and she checked the screen. "Your dad is taking you to dinner tomorrow night."

Now I was wide awake. "Why?"

"I know you're angry at him but you're going to have to work through your feelings—"

"Just Dad and me?" I asked. "No Claire, right?" A hint of desperation tinged my voice. My plan had been to distribute the posters and then finally be free of Claire. This plan did not involve going to dinner with her the very next evening.

"I don't know," Mom said. "He didn't mention her." She tapped at the phone screen.

The posters had been a masterstroke of evil genius, simple and diabolical:

FREE CHEESE!
CALL OR TEXT
USE PROMO CODE "GO AWAY"

Underneath I had printed Claire's personal cell phone number, which I had copied from Dad's phone months ago, knowing it would come in handy at some point.

"Oh, she *is* coming," Mom said, looking up from the text she'd just read.

My body went cold. My blood type was suddenly sub-zero terror. I had been confident that Claire would dump Dad once she started getting all those spam calls and texts. Claire would know I was responsible but wouldn't be able to prove it. And she would know that I would never stop until I got rid of her.

The alternative seemed almost impossible: that she liked Dad more than she disliked her phone blowing up with random strangers expecting cheese. No one could like my dad that much, especially if they've ever heard how loud he chews. I stared, glassy-eyed, imagining Claire smiling at Dad while he crunched his high-fiber cereal. Impossible!

What if Claire busted me in front of Dad tomorrow night? She'd probably make the whole thing sound like it was my fault.

A thin line of cold sweat broke out on my upper lip.

"Wow, you really are sleepy. I will definitely buy you a coffee." Mom was standing next to the car, holding my door open. Startled, I managed a smile as I got out and followed her into the mall.

"And then I need to find an outfit, okay? My old college roommate sent me a gift card and made me promise to find something that made me feel young and hot."

Could this get any more uncomfortable?

Mom saw the disgusted expression on my face. "Are you still upset about Claire coming to dinner? You're going to make the best of it, okay?"

"I wouldn't need to make the best of anything if Dad would just get his act together, dump her, and come back. I just want my old life back the way it was."

"Not me," she said softly, getting in line at the coffee shop. She leaned closer to me, a faint twinkle in her eye. "There are a million things I wish I could have changed about my life and my marriage, things I wish I had done differently. When you get to my age, what hurts the most is wondering how your life could have been."

We scooted up in line. The noise from the machines and the baristas gave us privacy.

"You wish you had a do-over," I said.

"No!" she replied, resting a hand on my shoulder. "That's what I'm trying to say. You are the reason I would never go back, even if I could, to change one thing. If I did, it might mean I didn't get to be your mom, and there's nothing on this planet I love more than you and being your mom. Dad and I made a lot of mistakes, but you are not one of them. You are the reason we can live with our mistakes."

The barista waved us forward and Mom ordered my soymilk latte. I really loved her.

Trying on a pair of high heels, Mom kept staring at her calves in the mirror like she had just discovered she had legs. Her cell phone buzzed again. She had ignored several calls so we could wrap up our shopping.

"Why high heels?" I asked. "You said the only time you ever used to wear stilettos is when you got a new haircut or a new man . . ."

I trailed off as Mom gave me a rueful little smile and a half-shrug.

A hand flew to my heart as my knees buckled. I sank onto the nearby bench and lowered my head between my knees to keep from hyperventilating. MOM HAD A DATE. She was buying sexy shoes because she had a date.

Just then, Mom's phone buzzed again and she answered.

"Excuse me?" she said after a moment. "Why would you think she had something to do with that?"

How could Mom do this to me? How could I fight a war on two fronts?

Mom tapped me on the shoulder. I looked up to see her pressing the phone to her chest, her frown now one of dark suspicion.

"Your father says that Claire has received more than a hundred prank calls and texts this afternoon."

"I am mute from shock," I said. "Tell Dad that." A poor defense but I was distracted.

"She's mute from shock. I don't think she had anything to do with it. No, she had a playdate right after school, then I picked her up."

My mom still said "playdate." So much was wrong with my life.

"No, then we came straight to the mall." Mom shifted the phone to her other ear, turning her back to me. Do parents think we can't hear when they do that? "I'm getting an outfit for a date with Charles. Yes, Charles from work. Well, he never liked you either."

She turned back to me and dropped the phone in her purse. "Sorry," she said. "I wanted to tell you about Charles earlier, but you were having such a hard time with Dad dating . . . . Honestly, though, now that Dad's with Claire and they seem to be getting serious, I've realized it's something we need to get used to. And me not dating, or keeping my dates a secret from you, won't help you adjust."

In all my misfortunes, do you see the common denominator? You're right: Claire. Without her, my life would have been back to normal by now.

I had to get rid of Claire and get my dad back

before Mom starting dating, too. It was time to gird my loins and toughen up. I was not going to back down until I had what I wanted, my real home with my real family.

When Mom was looking at a pair of heels that triggered my gag reflex, I closed my eyes and uttered a command to the hordes of strangers in Tess's neighborhood.

"Now is the hour! Go, my friends! Demand your cheese!"

CHAPTER 7

On Saturday evening, Dad arrived to take me to dinner. Separating the blinds in the front window, I saw Claire sitting in the passenger seat of his car. Cockroaches can live for weeks even after you've lopped their heads off, but this was extraordinary. I could not get rid of her!

The question now was: What was *her* plan?

Sliding into my seat, I fastened my seatbelt, feeling like I was strapping myself into a brand-new terrifying rollercoaster that no one had ever ridden. Mom walked back inside the house alone. I raised my hand to wave goodbye in case she turned back, but she didn't.

Dad turned and ruffled my hair before pulling out of the driveway. Attempting to smooth my hair back down, I looked at my window. The sun was slowly falling from the sky, like it was doing a death spiral for me.

Claire followed my gaze and smiled. "Beautiful sunset, isn't it?" Her face betrayed nothing. Either she didn't want to believe I was behind the cheese prank or she played a good game of cat-and-mouse.

"You know what a sunset means?" I asked, careful to sound casual as I took my first shot.

She turned around in her seat. "What?"

I lowered my chin and leaned forward, lowering my voice. "We have lost the protection of the light. Darkness returns to claim us now."

Her eyebrows flitted up briefly, then relaxed.

"Lizbeth," Dad warned. "I expect you to be on your best behavior tonight." He glanced at me in the rearview mirror and I smiled. Not a real smile, but like someone was pulling my ears back.

Claire glanced at me and winked, her eyes sparkling, her expression pleasant and plastic.

She knew.

She knew and she was coming for me.

"I picked the restaurant tonight," she said.

"Lizbeth, you're going to love it!" Dad exclaimed.

She rested a hand on his arm. "Of course she's

going to love it! Everyone loves cheese, right?" she cooed. "Have you ever been to a fondue restaurant, Lizbeth? The waiter brings you a big bowl of melted cheese and you dip fruit and bread into it."

I shifted in my seat. My back was sweating though my shirt.

"Cheese? That's it? That's the whole meal?" I asked.

She frowned. "Cheese isn't enough? Or is it too much? Do you think there's too much cheese in the world? Should we try to share it more evenly?"

There was blood in the water now. We both knew it.

Dad glanced over at her, then into the mirror, meeting my eyes again. He was having a hard time following this conversation. "I like cheese," he offered.

Neither of us responded to him. Claire obviously hadn't told him the full story.

Time to channel my own inner predator. Submerging, I circled for an attack. "I don't have time to worry about cheese. I'm focused on actual problems. By the way, I didn't know if Dad had broken up with you yet, but I wore my favorite shirt for you, just in case."

"That's sweet," she said. "A shirt with a poop emoji?"

"What? No! It's not a poop emoji. Gross!" I protested. "This is a chocolate kiss. This shirt is exactly how I see you."

It was a poop emoji. She knew, I knew, but Dad didn't.

Claire chuckled, her laugh sounding like someone had dropped a fork in a blender. "You are very thoughtful. And I have a surprise for you, too."

My eyebrows shot so high I could have tucked my hair behind them and used them as barrettes. "Really?"

"The restaurant manager is a dear friend of mine. I told him all about you and he insisted on preparing something very special just for you."

"Claire, you're the best!" Dad said. "What did I tell you, Lizbeth? She's the best, right?"

"She really is . . . something," I said, my eyes locked with Claire's.

"I hope you're hungry, Lizbeth," she said. "Because tonight you're going to get the biggest bowl of cheese you've ever seen. Knowing how much you love cheese, I expect you to eat every last bite."

The server took our drink orders and left. We all stared at each other, waiting for someone to start the conversation. Claire sat next to Dad but since we were in a small booth, she had been forced to put her purse next to me. She was careful to set it in plain view, zipped closed. Maybe Dad had told her about Margee.

Claire's shirt gaped open to reveal her collarbone and the mole on it. My eyes were glued to it. Did moles have roots or tendrils? Dad glanced at me, then realized what I was staring at. Claire shifted in her seat and gripped her shirt, closing it.

"If you cover that thing with duct tape," I said, "it will die off after a month or two."

Her cheeks turned red. "It's a mole, not a wart."

"There's no difference," I said.

"Of course there is!" she shot right back.

I leaned forward. "What is it, then?"

"Warts are a growth," she said with obvious distaste. "Moles are . . . a different kind of . . . growth." Her expression darkened. I'd won that point.

Dad's phone buzzed. "Ladies, I am sorry, but I promised the office I'd be around this weekend."

Claire sweetly waved him away as my insides screamed in panic. It was like watching helplessly as the safety glass lowered at the zoo's tiger enclosure. I was dead meat.

He was barely out of earshot when she leaned across the table. "You want to hear the strangest thing, Lizbeth?" she asked, her voice sing-song. "I had to drive around today and pull posters down from utility poles because someone put my number on a sign advertising free cheese."

"Your job as a lawyer is to put people in jail, right? Did you put anyone named Cheese in jail recently? Maybe those callers were asking you to free this individual known as Cheese."

Claire smiled grimly. "I'm not the kind of lawyer who puts people in jail."

"Oh. Well, that's good news for Mr. Cheese, I guess."

"You really don't like me dating your dad, do you?" She glanced at her purse, as if to make sure it was still safe.

"Don't complicate it," I said. "I don't like *you*. That's all."

The waiter arrived with our drinks and Claire settled back. "My parents divorced when I was in the sixth grade. I was angry, too. But I don't want you to waste years of your life being angry, like I did."

Sighing heavily, I looked around. Across from us, a couple flirted with each other, giggling. It made me feel weird. I didn't belong here. No. *Claire* didn't belong. That couple could have been my parents.

I turned my focus back to her. "I will never stop being angry at you. You need to break up with my dad. Tonight. Go ruin somebody else's life."

She cocked her head to one side, studying me. "Your parents didn't have the ending they wanted, I know. And I get how hard that is for you. But that doesn't mean we have to be enemies." She fanned out her fingers, as if trying to explain her feelings to someone who cared. "Imagine what could happen if you channeled your amazing energy toward creating your own happiness, instead of destroying ours. Life's not a fairy tale, even for the luckiest of us, but if you and I call a truce I think we can still have a pretty great story."

I pressed my palms flat on the table. "I don't want to be a part of your story."

She leaned forward again. Our noses were inches apart. *"We are all part of each other's stories."*

"Who's ready for fondue?!" We looked up

simultaneously as the server wheeled over a cart with a big bowl of melted cheese. Actually, *bowl* isn't the correct word. It was a cauldron.

Claire crossed her arms, a smug grin on her face. "I bet you want my help now."

I admit, the cauldron of cheese was an impressive power play.

"Want your help with what?" Dad said, returning to the table, then whistled when he saw the size of the bowl.

"Get your own, sweetheart," I said to her, my voice dripping with poisoned charm. "I'm going to eat every bite all by myself."

When I finished the cauldron of cheese, the manager came to our table to take a picture of me standing beside the empty bowl, with a grin on my face and my hands on my belly. I posed between Dad and Claire while the restaurant staff gathered around to snap their own photos.

"Oh, there's one thing I forgot to mention," I said, turning to Claire. "Dad probably forgot, too."

Claire shot a panicked look at Dad. He squinted, trying to remember what he had forgotten.

"I'm lactose intolerant."

CHAPTER 8

abruptly doubled over, one hand covering my mouth. On instinct, Claire angled away from me, clutching her purse on the other side of her body. This was perfect. It was almost unbelievable how well we worked together.

Moaning and lifting my arms weakly, I staggered toward her. She held her purse even farther away, her eyes flashing a warning.

"Mommy," I cried, "why do you love your purse more than me?"

Everyone in the restaurant switched their phones to film mode. "Stop it," she hissed.

"Hold me, mommyyy," I moaned, my arms flopping wildly, like a wounded baby bird crying for help.

"How could any mother choose a purse over her own child?" people murmured, voices low because no one likes loud audio on Facebook Live.

For the record, I'm not a monster. I only cosplay them. When I did finally hurl, it was outside, in the bushes, so her beloved purse was safe. The server even brought me a mint.

After a silent car ride home, Dad dropped me off, and I told Mom I was coming down with the stomach flu.

When I awoke Sunday morning, I had so much gas that I had to open a window. My butt was a trumpet of death. The stench was so strong and the explosions so deafening that I worried another fart might summon one of the four horsemen of the apocalypse. I wished I hadn't worn my favorite underwear to bed. The elastic hadn't been tested for these conditions.

Dad's voice startled me. He was downstairs. I stood very still, listening.

"She needs more structure," he said. "Discipline."

Sneaking into the hallway, I stood very still to eavesdrop.

"Discipline didn't cause her problems, so discipline won't fix them," Mom replied. "What she needs is help processing all these changes. We should sit down with her and talk about everything she's going through, and why she's having a hard time lately. Maybe we should look for a family therapist . . ." Dad must have given her a dark look because she immediately added, "I'm not trying to start a fight, okay?"

I almost felt bad about last night. I was trying to get rid of Claire, not make trouble for Mom. Revenge was a weapon that was hard to aim.

"*Talk*. Good grief," Dad said. "That's all you ever want to do. Talking can't fix everything!"

"No," Mom said. "But it's a lot more useful than silence! And you know what else is useful? Listening! You should try it!"

"Oh, and here I thought that you didn't want to start a fight." He was snippy.

"When are you going to grow up?" Mom said, her voice sounding thin and stretched. "I am not trying to make you seem like the bad guy! I just want you to seem like a father!"

It was silent for a long time. I chewed the inside of my lip.

"I know this is incredibly awkward," another woman's voice said. "I'm so sorry."

CLAIRE WAS IN MY HOUSE.

I had to get closer. I took a step down the stairs, my back against the wall. Claire was sitting on MY couch. Mom handed her a cup of tea. And a cookie!

Shutting my eyes tight, I prayed not to scream. Opening them, I took another step forward to spy on Dad, who was sitting next to Claire.

"Look, I agree that counseling is probably a good idea," he said. "But we might need to think bigger than that. Lizbeth is convinced that breaking up Claire and me will solve her problems. If she continues on this path, we're going to have to take a new approach."

Silently, I lifted my foot to take another step. Wait. Which step had that awful wheeze-creak?

"And by *a new approach*, you mean?" Mom asked.

Holding my breath, I racked my memory. Which step was it?

"We'll have to reevaluate our arrangement, that's what I mean," he said.

My foot hung in midair.

"You mean custody?" Mom asked.

"Claire and I have been talking about moving in together. Maybe Lizbeth would do better in a two-parent household."

My hands flew up to my mouth to silence my gasp. Losing my balance, I tumbled down the last five stairs, landing smack on my butt. I farted, too, just from the shock of the landing.

Mom rushed over and checked my limbs to see if they were broken. Dad got his phone out, frantically asking if he should dial 911. Claire remained on the couch, eyes wide.

Mom released me as I stood. In the hope of reclaiming some of my dignity, I cleared my throat. "I just came downstairs for a glass of water." Calmly hobbling to the kitchen, I took a glass from the cabinet, filled it, and tried to drink it before my shaking hands sloshed all the water out. All three adults watched, dumbstruck.

"Now, where were you?" I asked, turning to face them. "Oh, yes. Custody. Whether any of us like it or not, I live here now. I live with Mom. And Dad?" I looked at him. "You're fighting *over* me, not *for* me. I know the difference. It's too late to win me back."

"Too late?" he echoed. He tried to force a smile; but I saw the tremors at the corners of his mouth. "Hey, we believe in time travel and Einstein-Rosen bridges! In our world there is no such thing as too late."

"That used to be true. Then you left." I looked down at my toes, wiggling them to keep from crying. "And my world changed."

I marched back upstairs. For the record, it's the fourth step.

After slamming the door to my room, I decided to stay busy by working on my supernova project for science class. I had done all the research already, though, and it didn't take very long to write a script for the presentation. I had even printed some pictures while I was at Tess's house, and now I carefully cut out each separate image to put on a poster board later. I then moved on to dumping everything out of my backpack and cleaning it out for the new week. Crumpling trash is cathartic. My hand closed around a piece of scribbled-on paper, and just before I smushed it, I caught sight of what was typed on it.

THIS IS YOUR SECOND DISCIPLINE SLIP

The walls shrank and spun. What had I done?

My eyes darting from side to side, I tried to think. I remembered practicing Mom's signature and making notes about where to improve. I remembered tucking the practice paper in my backpack.

In the same pocket as the discipline slip.

I had turned in the practice paper.

"Before you send me to the office," I said to Ms. Farris on Monday morning, "can we both agree that my penmanship was extraordinary? In cursive. That should count for something."

She was sipping a mug of coffee, which seemed unusually large even for the first day of the school week.

"Do you have the actual discipline slip?" she asked. Her voice was a monotone, like the automated voices on computer programs.

My gulp of dread echoed off the walls as I rifled through my backpack and produced the correct slip. Handing it to her, she lifted both pieces of paper into the air, comparing the samples.

"Well, you are right," she said, lowering the papers. "Unfortunately, I have to refer you to the principal's office. She's going to call your mother for a meeting."

I returned to my seat. Resting my face on my forearms, I tried slowly breathing in and out. My toes were numb. My stomach was a pit of ice. My nerves were on fire. Terror is a multifaceted experience. This is something most horror movies do not adequately convey.

When I was sure no one was watching I pulled out my journal. I needed to prepare my defense. However, my only advocates, the people who could vindicate my decision, were a former president and Jesus. It occurred to me now that both men had been assassinated. I found this troubling.

Until now, my problems at this new school had been misunderstandings. Today, however, I had been caught in a clear and deliberate violation of ethics. I could not expect mercy.

What's the difference between a sixth-grader who has been caught cheating and an onion? A principal will cry over the onion.

While I was preoccupied with my guilt spiral, Ms. Farris passed around the sign-up sheet for the talent show. When it reached our pod, the four of us stared at it.

"Band, lip sync, dance, piano, magic act . . ." Tess read the entries out loud. "Marcos is going to saw his little sister in two."

I raised my eyebrows.

"It's the only trick he does really well," Joseph said, sounding bored. "She has a twin."

"Are you still in?" Paul asked me.

I hesitated, holding the paper. Ms. Farris caught

my eye, motioning for me to write my name down and pass it on. My shoulders slumped. Unfortunately, being a delinquent did not disqualify me from participating in the talent show. "I'm in," I confirmed to my pod-mates.

"What do we write down for our talent?" Joseph asked, grabbing the paper.

Tess's face brightened. "How about . . . art? We're starting our art unit today anyway. We can use class time to work on our project."

The art, music, and PE classes rotated every six weeks, so this was the first day of a new session of art. Perhaps the Universe was sending us a signal.

"Brilliant." Joseph wrote *ART* on the sign-up sheet next to our names.

"Easy for you to say," said Paul. "You can draw and paint. I can't."

"Art can be a lot of things," Tess assured him. "Pottery. Sculptures. Fabrics!"

"Oh yeah, you've tapped into my skill set now," said Paul sarcastically.

"What about," said Tess, ignoring his skepticism, "a scale model of SuperChicken!"

Joseph shook his head, scowling. "I think it's too soon to unveil him."

Tess instantly deflated. "You're right. What does our feathered champion have going for him except for the element of surprise?" She was really nuts about that comic.

Joseph nudged her. "He has you, Tess. He's a very lucky chicken."

"You encourage this?" I said to Joseph.

Tess sighed. "Where do we even start with you, Lizbeth? Encouragement is what real friends do." She turned to Joseph. "Do you ever feel like we spend half our time explaining things to her?"

Later that morning, my classmates and I shuffled through the halls to my first art class at Plains Creek Middle School.

The room was brightly lit with lots of space between tables, letting little reflections of light bounce off the linoleum everywhere. A mural on one wall had what looked like an exploding word flower until I peered closer and realized it said *Teach Peace*. Both words used the same middle letters. I cocked my head, intrigued that the two words had so much in common.

Around the letters were posters showing pictures of doves, peace symbols, sunrises, even a bull in a dark meadow and some orange dancers. Peace looks different to everyone, I guess. My version was a Friday night movie with Mom and Dad and a jar of Marshmallow Fluff for dinner. I didn't get either of those anymore, though. Mom got worried that Marshmallow Fluff dinners could be used as evidence against her if things ever got ugly. I struggled to see how marshmallows could be forced to testify, though. Divorce is so weird.

Mr. Westchester sat behind his desk. He didn't say hello as we filed in, but he motioned toward some cardboard boxes stacked on a back table. Each box had a name written on it. My classmates grabbed their boxes, scattered to the worktables— where pod-mates reconvened like separated magnets snapping back together—and started unpacking art supplies. I glimpsed sticky glue bottles, stubby colored pencils, crusted-over watercolor paint kits, and multitudes of scrap paper. Mr. Westchester propped his feet up on his desk, watching.

"Excuse me," I said. "I'm new." I pointed at my name tag. "I don't have an art supply box."

Mr. Westchester pointed arbitrarily at Paul.

"You can share. We're just doing a warm-up exercise today."

"Actually," I said, "my pod-mates and I are doing an art project for the talent show. We kind of hoped we could start working on that."

Mr. Westchester looked skeptical. "What kind of art project?"

"That's . . . to be determined," I said.

"I see." He appeared unimpressed. "Why choose art for your talent?"

"Maybe art chose us," Tess suggested, looking at her sneakers. She wore different colored socks on each foot today.

"We can tell him the truth, Tess," Joseph said. He squared his narrow shoulders and looked Mr. Westchester in the eye. "No one wants us in their talent show act. All we've got is each other, and none of us can even do anything. Art is the only thing that makes sense."

Our classmates looked down or away from us, as if it was embarrassing for someone to actually admit there was a pecking order determining our daily humiliations.

"So in other words," said Mr. Westchester slowly, "if you don't have a talent, you might as well do art?"

Joseph glanced nervously at the rest of us. "This feels like a trick question."

Paul sighed, and Mr. Westchester's gaze settled on him. "Look, I don't know how to do art," Paul said. "But the whole point of the talent show is to raise money so we can keep the art and music classes, right? They're cutting the arts because standardized tests can't score creativity. You can't get an A in wonder. But if you see the news, you realize that's what's missing in the world. So . . . why *wouldn't* we choose art for our project?"

This was the most I'd ever heard Paul say in one gulp.

Mr. Westchester rested his chin on his hands. He didn't seem angry or bored. He seemed like he was actually thinking. Tess finished emptying her supply box and began organizing. Paul and Joseph and I stayed awkwardly still, waiting. The rest of the class seemed to be ignoring us for the moment, though it was hard to be sure.

"You have two choices," he finally said. "I can teach you the basic principles of art and help you make a great project for the show. Or, I can help you become artists. Once you become an artist, you're an artist for life. But those two things are very different, so I need to know right now which one you prefer."

"Which one gets more chicks?" Joseph asked. Tess and I threw our hands over our faces, groaning.

"Which one is harder?" Paul asked.

"Being an artist," Mr. Westchester promptly replied. "Every day, you try to create beauty for a world that celebrates cruelty. Every day, you choose between protecting yourself and being true to your work." He raised his eyebrows. "Here be dragons, as they say."

He was a nerd, too! *Here be dragons* was written on maps long ago to warn people about traveling into uncharted lands.

He started chewing a cuticle.

"Excuse me," Joseph said, "but 'dragons' is a metaphor, right?" His face looked slightly pale. "Reptiles carry salmonella."

"Let's do the hard thing," Paul said, looking at Tess, Joseph, and me. We all agreed.

"Okay. You can start right now." Clapping his hands and standing, he spoke to the class as a whole. "Everybody grab a piece of paper and something to draw with. I don't care what you use: pen, pencil, marker."

We all scrambled to follow his instructions.

"Now, close your eyes and picture a cartoon dog, the silliest one you can. What do his ears look like, his nose, his tail? When you have a complete picture of him, nod."

I nodded. Mine was partially inspired by the ill-fated Potatoes, before he got mashed.

"Open your eyes," Mr. Westchester said. "Now, draw what you saw. Exactly as you saw it. Try to make every detail on that paper match what you saw in your head."

I tried a couple of times before crumpling up the paper in embarrassment.

"Lizbeth," said Mr. Westchester, "why did you do that?"

"The picture in my head was different," I said. "It was so much better."

One by one, my classmates finished. None of them seemed eager to show their work either. The atmosphere in the room was heavy with disappointment.

"That's your first lesson." Mr. Westchester folded his arms, watching us for a reaction.

"What?" Tess exclaimed. "We didn't learn anything. You just let us all fail and feel dumb."

Mr. Westchester studied Tess. She fidgeted in her chair, but her eyes lit with anger. She was so protective of us.

"I taught you that the work you create will never look exactly like the picture in your head. Make your peace with that now," he said. "You can't make art—you can't even make it to adulthood—unless you accept that nothing turns out exactly as you imagined. And that's okay. Keep going anyway."

Mr. Westchester fished around in his pocket and pulled out some coins that he counted as he spoke. "Look, you all gave up because the result didn't match your expectation. And what I want you to consider is that your expectation was the real problem, not your result."

We looked at each other, and then people started holding their drawings up for others to see. I had to admit, I liked a lot of the other drawings. Of course, I didn't know what the artists had originally wanted, but what they ended up with was cool.

"If you judge anything, even yourself, by expectations," Mr. Westchester said, "you'll always be unhappy. So, for today, your assignment is to take your picture home and enjoy it. Personally, I happen to really like each of them."

The bell rang. It was time to switch classes. "Now get out of here," he said, standing up. "I've got a free period next, and I have just enough money for the vending machine in the teacher's lounge."

CHAPTER 9

I sat on a wooden bench outside the principal's office waiting on Mom to arrive. I jiggled one foot, wondering what happened in these meetings. Did the kid get to talk, or only the adults? Would everyone be angry? Would there be refreshments?

A middle-aged woman pushed a rolling trash can past me. I had never met her, but obviously, she was the janitor. And I knew the janitor had an incredible voice, a gift that she hid from the world.

Parking the trash can, she eased herself down to sit next to me, then put one hand on her lower back, stretching.

I leaned toward her. "How long have you known?" I whispered.

"Excuse me?" She turned to look at me, pretending to be confused.

"It's all right," I said in my most soothing, quiet voice. "Your secret is safe with me. Not everyone can understand these things."

I stretched out beside her, straightening my legs and then crossing them at the ankles. "Tell me something," I said. We were just two kindred spirits sharing a moment. "Did you ever dream of the stage?"

She stood, a look of irritation on her face. She grabbed the trash can and shoved it violently down the hall. I jumped up to call her back, but at that moment Joseph came around the corner. He slammed right into me, knocking me over.

My palms skidded across the tile floor as I tried to catch myself. I scrambled back to my feet, but he didn't even stop to apologize.

"Don't tell Paul you saw me!" he called over his shoulder, racing in the direction of the nurse's office. One hand was covering his nose.

I wiped my dirty palms on my pants, shaking my head. Those older boys were bullying Joseph—I had already figured that out. But why would Joseph hide from Paul? If I didn't get suspended for my forgery, I wanted to learn the answer.

"Lizbeth? You okay?"

I whirled around to see Dad.

"Where's Mom?" I demanded.

"Are you sure you're all right?" Dad asked, stepping closer.

"Where's Mom?" I repeated, ignoring him. "I want Mom." Actually, I wanted Dad to wrap his arms around me, but I stepped away from him. I didn't even know why. I was stuck in a weird dance with him these days. When he moved closer, I moved away. And when I wanted to get close, he wasn't there.

It was as if our music had changed. Divorce had been our family song suddenly ending, and none of us could find the rhythm of the new one.

"Your mom couldn't leave work early, so I came instead. Look," Dad said, reaching for my hand, "I know you don't believe in time travel anymore. But do you believe in second chances? Could you still believe in those?"

Gnawing on my lower lip, I studied the ground a minute, and then nodded. He wrapped his arms around me and I rested my head against his stomach. Maybe he was a jerk, but he was my jerk.

I looked up at him. "Could you give Mom a second chance too?"

He sighed. "Honey, we've been over this so many

times in the last two years. Your mom and I aren't going to get back together. But that doesn't mean—"

Just then, Paul came around the corner, frowning, carrying Joseph's lunch bag.

"Hey!" I said, holding out a hand to stop him. "Joseph had to go to the nurse. I think his nose is bleeding!"

"He's still in the building?" Paul looked around. "He didn't leave?" He stormed past me in the direction of the nurse's office.

A moment later, Ms. Camp emerged into the hallway. "Lizbeth, I'm ready for you. And you must be Lizbeth's father?"

This was my first time standing before a principal under these conditions. Usually I was accepting an award. Panicked, acting on pure instinct, I thrust out my hand. "It's an honor to be here."

"You think this is funny?" Ms. Camp asked.

"Ms. Camp," Dad intervened, stepping in front of me, "Lizbeth always says the wrong thing when she's nervous. Boy, could I tell you stories."

After studying him for a moment, she finally smiled. "I'm sure you're aware of the challenges our school is facing this year," she said, gesturing for us to follow her into the office. "Which is why I really need your daughter to focus her creative energy on something other than breaking school rules."

Before we followed her inside, Dad rested one hand on my shoulder and whispered in my ear. "Let me handle this, okay? And when we're done, I think you and I need to talk." He didn't sound angry. He sounded protective and concerned, like my old Dad.

Maybe everything would be okay. Still, I tucked my hand in my pocket, just to keep it safe from accepting any more imaginary awards.

We sat at a picnic table in the park. The weather was beautiful, with a bright fall sun and the red and orange leaves dangling above us. A cool breeze swept by, making the trees shimmy and dance. Dad and I each had blue slushies. In between slurps, we tried to make each other laugh by wiggling the straw up and down, making screechy noises.

"So . . . why can't you give Mom a second chance?" I asked.

"Because she doesn't need one," he answered. "She didn't do anything wrong."

"So *she* needs to give *you* a second chance?" I asked. "I can talk to her."

"No. No, I left. She didn't kick me out." He set his slushy down and looked into the distance, rubbing his chin. "She deserves a great husband. But I'm terrible at it."

"So you just gave up on us?"

"No," he replied, his voice sad. "I gave up on me." He pinched the bridge of his nose. "Listen, peaches. I know you don't like Claire."

I shrugged.

"I need you to stop attacking her. She's having . . . digestive trouble from the stress of trying to make friends with you. That's not really very fair to her, now, is it?"

I smiled, jumped up, ran around the table and gave Dad a big kiss on the cheek.

He laughed. "Okay, apology accepted."

Except it wasn't an apology. I was thanking him.

Now I knew her weakness.

Inside the grocery store Tuesday evening, Mom stared at the row of vitamins. She picked one up, read the label, set it back, picked up another.

"Aren't they all the same brand?" I said, exasperated.

"Yes, but this one is for people under stress," she said, lifting a box to show me the label, "and that one is for active adults."

"Which one are you?"

"Exactly," she murmured, reaching for a third option.

Out of the corner of my eye, I spotted a tuft of hair, like the wing of a bat. No! It could not be! But it was.

Claire was pushing a shopping cart through the store. She nearly hit a toddler who was making a dash for the cookies, but Claire was so busy texting with one hand that she didn't notice. Her cart had a screeching wheel, and as she pushed it slowly past us, I realized the Universe had granted me a perfect opportunity for vengeance. A plan formed in my mind with dizzying speed.

"Mom, can I go see if any cereal is on sale?" I tried to sound casual, but a slight tremor in my voice almost betrayed me. Thankfully, Mom was utterly overwhelmed with nutritional decisions. "I'll be right back."

She waved me off, still concentrating on the vitamin labels. Did she want strong bones or a good mood? Was she stretched too thin or an on-the-go woman? Was she too old for chewables?

I couldn't let Claire see me. She was smart for an idiot, so I had to be extra sneaky.

I quickly found just what I needed. After scooping several boxes of Extra Strength Gas Busters into my arms, I sneaked down to the end of my row and peeked around the corner.

She stood with her back to me in front of the dairy case. She had parked her cart by the baked goods table, so a display of donuts was blocking her view of me. This was like taking candy from a baby, except that taking candy from a baby would be mean.

Approaching the cart, I crouched down, reached up with one hand, and scooted a few items to one side. After creating a suitable funnel, I dropped my payload into the hole, one box at a time, then covered the items with her other groceries.

I straightened and walked away. Not only was she preoccupied with her phone, she didn't know me well enough to recognize me from the back.

And may it ever be so.

Turning down an aisle, I spied another product that caught my eye. I hesitated, weighing my odds. How far could I go? How badly did I want her gone?

I grabbed it and backtracked. As soon as her back was turned, I casually strolled past and dropped the item in.

Inspired, I set off in search of the most embarrassing products the store sold. Playing a cloak-and-dagger spy drama with personal care products really gets your pulse racing. That screeching wheel made it easy to track her through the store.

I was slowly backing away from Claire's cart after dropping another item in when I bumped into Mom.

"There you are!" she said. "Where's the cereal?"

I held one finger to my lips, nudging her and her cart backwards down the aisle, out of sight.

"It wasn't on sale," I whispered, trying to steady my breath.

"Why are you whispering?"

"Who's whispering?" I whispered. "Oh! I am." I cleared my throat. "So, which vitamin won?" I asked, wiping my forehead with the back of my hand. Covert operations can be surprisingly sweaty.

Mom slowly turned the cart, and we walked down the aisle. Glancing behind us, I confirmed that

Claire was not following. The screeching was silent. But she was still out there, lurking. We had to escape before she cornered us. My heartbeat pounded in my ears.

"I decided on the vitamins that support healthy hair, skin, and nails. I suppose it's time for me to freshen up the advertising, if you know what I mean." In case I didn't, she winked and added a little sashay to her walk.

I gagged.

She pretended not to notice. My heart was still beating wildly. I concentrated on listening for the screech.

Mom was studying the dizzying array of soup cans when I heard it. *Screech.* The dreaded thing was near. But which direction was it headed?

"Lizbeth." The voice came from behind me.

My spine suddenly felt like it was made of freezing cold steel. My arms went limp and my knees quaked with fear. I couldn't force myself to turn and see. It was like that feeling when your brain wakes up before your body does, and you can't move.

"I knew it had to be you," Claire said. Wheeling her cart next to ours, she began throwing packages into our cart. "I do not need extra strength gas busters," she hissed, "and I certainly don't need three packages of it."

"Yeah! My dad said you need a lot more!"

She folded her arms, and her eyes became narrow slits of fire as she spoke slowly, spitting out each word like a sour grape. "Why do I even try to be nice to you?"

"Let's be honest," I said in my no-nonsense voice. "You only care about my dad, not me."

"That's not true. I've really been hoping we could be friends."

"Liar liar pants on fire! Hope those things are nonflammable!"

"Lizbeth," Mom asked, looking between us both, "what is going on?"

"You mean the adult diapers you put in my cart?" Claire asked, tossing a mega pack into our cart with a savage *thwump*. "And the nose hair trimmer?" *Plunk*, right in our cart. "And prescription-strength deodorant for extreme body odor?" *Whump*. "Mouthwash for unbearably bad breath?" *Thwump*. "And athlete's foot spray for the fungus that just won't die?" *Whump*.

Her upper body strength was impressive. "Are you sure you don't need those?" I said weakly.

Mom grabbed me by the shoulder, her fingers like talons digging into my skin. "Did you put those things in her cart?"

"I was only trying to be helpful. How else is she going to get a new boyfriend after Dad dumps her?"

"Why weren't you watching her?" Claire said to Mom. "Lizbeth seems to be lacking in adult supervision, at least when she's with you."

"Don't you ever question my abilities as her mother," Mom snapped, her eyes blazing.

Gulping, I took a step back. My mom rarely loses her temper, but when she does, she breathes fire. Her fury could level entire cities. Godzilla probably has a poster of my mom on his bedroom wall.

"Well, unless you approve of this behavior," Claire sputtered, "she owes me an apology."

"Let's see," Mom said. "Should she apologize that you stink? Or have such thick nose hair that Bigfoot sightings have been reported in there? Or that she doesn't like you dating her dad? Or maybe she just doesn't like *you*."

Claire's mouth fell open but she just stood there.

Customers were slowly filing past, stealing glances at us, a few pretending to be looking at their phones but clearly trying to get a video.

Claire and I sure have made some memories together.

Mom grabbed my hand and pulled me out of the store. I wanted to look back at the destruction left in our wake but couldn't.

In the parking lot, we sat in the car in silence for a long moment before Mom spoke. "So, I didn't behave very well back there. We both need to work on how we treat Claire."

"I personally think we both nailed it," I said. "And she deserved worse."

"Why do you think that?" Mom asked. Her voice was calm, but her cheeks were bright pink so I knew she was still mad.

Adults are always so slow to see the big picture. "Because she's standing in the way of everything we want," I answered.

"No, she's not," Mom replied. "There is a big difference between someone blocking your path and someone crossing your path." After a deep breath, she continued. "She is just crossing our path. She can't give us what we want so there's no reason to be mean to her."

"If she broke up with Dad, we would have a chance to be a family again. Even if you and Dad didn't get back together, we could at least all live together. I mean, think of how much money it would save! I'm not even saying you have to love him."

She looked at me, tears in her eyes. "I do love him, honey. I always will. That's why I fought to hold on to him, and that's why I finally let him go."

I stared out the window, and after a while I started thinking about Sydney. She treated me like I was blocking her only path to happiness. And what about the boys who were mean to Joseph? Maybe all people in the world were trying to solve their problems by hurting other people. If that was true, we were one messed-up planet. With a lot of unsolved problems.

Of course, in the midst of these deep thoughts, I had forgotten the most important thing on my agenda that day. Which, as it turns out, wasn't humiliating Claire. My supernova project was due tomorrow, and I didn't have any poster board.

CHAPTER 10

In the morning, before the first bell rang, I raced to the art room. My whole body was vibrating from nerves. I was already tense about the class project; I hadn't planned on committing a crime, too.

I crept into Mr. Westchester's dark classroom. After checking that I was alone, I hit the lights and headed to a supply closet in the back corner. Hands shaking, I opened the door and found the larger supplies stored inside.

Along with a stack of newspaper clippings.

Mr. Westchester was staring at me. From a clipping. An article from a newspaper, the edges neat and the corners sharp. Someone had been careful cutting it out. The thin paper shook in my unsteady hands as I read.

Martin Westchester, son of famed heart surgeon Clyde Westchester, will host a viewing
of his new collection of paintings, "Scenes
in Gray," tomorrow night at the Village Art
House. Mr. Westchester's art has been featured in numerous gallery exhibitions and
national magazines. *Art America* recently
named him one of the "Top Painters Under
30" in the world.

On the back was a Post-It note that read, *Your
father would have been so proud. Mom.* I turned the clipping back over to check the date on the article. Two
years ago.

Mr. Westchester was a famous artist. Wow. So
why was he here, teaching art in a school district
that didn't care about art? Did everyone know how
famous he had been, and maybe still was? Being the
new kid means you can never be sure what's a startling new revelation. You're always walking in halfway through the movie.

"What are you doing?"

I whirled around. A very real Mr. Westchester stood in the doorway. He speed-walked across
the room and took the clipping from my hands.

Crumpling it into a ball, he dropped it on the floor, his eyes never leaving mine.

My heart pounded but my hand was already on a poster board. I lifted it up as if this was an explanation. "Borrowing this?"

"*Borrowing* implies you will return it in the same condition. Were you going to write on it?"

I nodded, ashamed.

"Then you're stealing." He stared me down, his expression unreadable. "You know the school's in danger of losing its funding for the arts program. If I write you up for this, you could be kicked out of my class. You might never have another chance to take an art class. And in the meantime, what would you do for the talent show?"

"I'm sorry!" I said in desperation. "Please don't give me a discipline slip. I'm new here and I'm under a lot of stress and my dad wants me to move in with a . . . a . . ." Lacking any other suitable word, I exclaimed, "a lawyer!"

Mr. Westchester almost laughed before he pressed his lips together tightly. "Tell you what, Lizbeth . . ." He did a double-take. "Why are you still wearing that name tag?"

"I have to," I replied, feeling the air get sucked

out of my lungs. As if this conversation wasn't humiliating enough. "Until Ms. Farris says I can take it off."

"Uh, okay. Well, I'll make you a deal." He turned back to his desk, picked up a clay mug full of colored pencils, and held it out to me. "Some people say sixth-graders are not capable of real art, not at this age—"

"Of course we are!" My eyebrows collided as I grimaced at that outrageous statement. I'd seen middle-school students dominate cons with their own homemade costumes and accessories. I myself have never been gifted with a sewing machine or papier-mâché, but I like to think that sabotaging one's father's girlfriends is also an art form.

"Prove it. Pick a color. Pick one that makes your heart feel something."

Panicking, I grabbed the first colored pencil that caught my eye, a medium blue.

"With your future in the arts on the line, I would've expected you to choose something a little more interesting, but we can work with this," he said. "Why do people say they're feeling blue, when what they're really feeling is sad? What does the color blue mean to them?"

Twisting my lips from side to side, I tried to think. In anime, hair color tells you a lot about the character. White or gray is used for wise mentors. Red is for troublemakers or hyper characters. Blue is usually for people with magical or mystical powers, or sometimes just very smart characters. Colors are a signal to the audience. I'd never thought about what colors might signal to us in real life. Except for beige. Beige is the color of walls that you don't want to see.

Mr. Westchester checked his watch. "Sixty seconds. If you need to think aloud, it won't count against you."

"Um, it's the color of the sky," I murmured. "And the ocean."

He leaned against his desk, setting the mug of colored pencils back down. "Keep going. Why would the sky or the ocean make people sad?"

"Well . . . to look at the sky, I have to tilt my head up. And with the ocean, I have to squint my eyes to see all the way to the horizon. I can't see the end or the edges of either one. They're huge. I can only see a little bit at a time. Because they are so much bigger than I am."

He waited.

"I've got it," I blurted. "Blue is the color of sadness because the sky and the ocean go on forever . . . but they go on without us."

The silence in the air seemed different now, as if an invisible door was opening. Mr. Westchester held my gaze. "We're feeling loneliness?"

"Maybe?" I chewed on my lower lip for a second, then shook my head. "Or maybe we feel small, like we don't matter much. And people really want to matter, more than anything." Now it made sense that mystical characters would have blue hair. Blue connected us to the bigger, unseen world.

"Do we?" Mr. Westchester asked, sounding genuinely curious, like he wasn't talking to a bratty, thieving kid but to another adult. I stood up straighter. "Do you really want to matter, Lizbeth?"

"Sure," I said. "But . . ." I decided to trust him with my doubts. "If we're talking about the whole world, why would one person matter?"

"Maybe that's why people get sad," he said, a kind light in his eyes. "They don't have an answer to that. But I think that's what art can help you figure out." He smiled. "Take the poster board and go. You earned it."

My heart beat faster, as if the blank poster board

was a question waiting to be answered. Suddenly I didn't want to pick it up, even if it was just for a class project.

If art was going to tell me why I mattered, art might also tell me why I didn't. Art might tell me why it had been so easy for my dad to walk away, why it was so easy for Sydney to hurt my feelings. Maybe this was going to be the most dangerous classroom experiment of all.

"That's one more reason I feel confident about you," Mr. Westchester said.

I looked up at him, confused.

"Anyone who hesitates before a blank page, a canvas, or in this case, a poster board—anyone who pauses before rushing in to fill the silence—that person is capable of art."

He pointed at the clock on the wall. "Better get to class. And do me a favor—don't tell anyone about that newspaper clipping."

⌖

"Sit next to me," Hailey said as we walked into homeroom. "You can tell me what I'm supposed to do for our presentation while Ms. Farris takes roll."

Pursing my lips, I exhaled slowly, trying to steady my nerves. Back home, presenting projects in class had always been easy for me. But I'd never had an entire friendship riding on the outcome.

At my locker, I'd hastily decorated the poster board with the supernova pictures I had already printed, and on the back, I'd pasted a copy of Hailey's lines along with their cues. I slid into Sydney's empty seat and unrolled the poster, pointing out the cues to Hailey. She hadn't wanted to practice beforehand, but I had made everything so easy that I figured she didn't need to.

Suddenly the room around us got quiet, and it seemed like everyone was holding their breath, waiting for something terrible to happen. Hailey and I looked up, mystified.

Sydney had walked in. She was wearing a wrinkled red shirt. Her hair wasn't in braids or a ponytail, either, and it even had a little frizz. The corners of her mouth were turned down. She looked like her heart was sinking and she was struggling to stay afloat.

Sydney pointed at me. I felt like a butterfly pinned, still alive, to a display board.

"What is she doing in my seat?" Sydney hissed.

"Lizbeth," Ms. Farris murmured, "go back to your regular seat, please."

I stood, trying to make a big arc around and away from Sydney. Sydney's eyes swept over to the rest of her clique, who were all dressed in pink. She looked down at her wrinkled red shirt, then shot a glare at Hailey. I slid into my seat next to Paul, who gave me a *What did you expect?* side-eye.

Hailey shrugged and looked away. "Oops," she said, pulling a hairbrush from her bag. "I forgot to text you. The football team is wearing red today so we're wearing pink."

As if on cue, a horde of red-shirted boys swarmed past the door on the way to the morning's pep rally, shoving each other and laughing.

Sydney stood there, a blank look in her eyes. I wanted to comfort her, tell her it probably had been an honest mistake. She turned her eyes toward me, noticing my pink shirt. Her eyes changed from blank canvases to cold anger.

"Why is LivesWet wearing pink?" Sydney pointed to me but looked at Hailey.

Hailey smiled. "She's my partner for the project."

Sydney cleared her throat as she sat in her chair. I wondered if she was trying not to cry.

Hailey hit all her lines in our presentation like a pro. She spoke clearly and with appropriate volume.

"Hailey and Lizbeth, your hard work paid off," Ms. Farris said, giving us an A.

"Thank you," Hailey chirped.

I turned to high-five her. She smiled vaguely at me and walked back to her seat. Did she remember our deal? I was her friend now.

Tess leaned toward me across the table as soon as I sat down. "You're not going to say anything?"

"About what?" My heart was still pounding. The trial by fire was over but somehow my body didn't know yet.

"You did all the work," she said. "I know you did. Hailey can't even spell the word *supernova*."

Joseph sighed and went back to scribbling in the margins of his paper.

My euphoria floated away like a balloon the wind had stolen. "You don't understand," I whispered, swallowing. This was supposed to be a celebratory moment. Everything had gone so well! My plan had worked!

"Nah, *you* don't understand." Paul was still giving

me the side-eye. "You don't need them. You already have friends."

"Why can't I have lots of friends?" I asked, frowning.

"You can," Tess said. "We don't care."

"But they do," Joseph added.

My head started to throb and I slumped down in my chair. The problem was that I had picked Hailey as my new best friend. Obviously, she didn't like me very much, but that was no reason we couldn't make it work. That was exactly what I'd been trying to communicate to Mom and Dad for the past two years. If you were meant to be together, you had to make it work.

Trying to steady my lunch tray, I walked up behind Hailey. Was Sydney going to let me sit with the group? Or was she going to rip me to shreds for even trying? My hands gripping the tray made the shaking worse, and my pudding cup started to wiggle over to the edge. Any second it was going to leap to its death.

Sydney turned and seemed surprised to see me standing there.

"Sorry," I said, although I didn't know what I was sorry for. It just seemed to be the expected response when a mean girl looked at you.

Sydney sat next to Hailey, and neither scooted over to make room for me. My heart pounded. I wasn't sure what to do.

"What?" said Hailey. She sounded somewhere between confused and irritated.

"I thought we were friends?" I said, trying to sound perky, not accusing.

"And?"

"I thought that meant I could sit with you? At lunch?" I felt so small, as if I had crumpled my dignity into a ball and tossed it at a wastebasket. And missed by a mile.

Sydney started to say something to Hailey, but Hailey cut her off. "She's the reason I got an A."

"She is a very hard worker," Lucy added, "even if she is annoying."

"Look at it this way," Hailey said to Sydney. "Lizbeth can do a ton of our work for us. You won't feel rushed to get caught up on our homework."

"I didn't agree to that!" I was so startled that my hands slipped.

The pudding cup landed on Sydney's shoulder,

then tumbled down her sleeve and splattered across the table. Everyone watched in horror as it grew mercifully still.

"Sorry!" I think everyone heard me swallow. I definitely heard them breathing through their open mouths. We were all in shock.

Except for Tess. She was facedown on the table, shoulders shaking. Joseph watched and just shook his head.

Sydney blinked, strangely calm. Several people handed her napkins as she wiped her sleeve. Hailey watched with narrowed eyes, as if waiting to see if Sydney would make another scene.

"Interesting fact about pudding," I said, trying to ease the tension. "Pudding used to be sausage." I looked around the table for support. There was none. "You couldn't tell if it was going to be any good till you bit through it, so that's why we say the proof is in the pudding." I cleared my throat. "Fascinating, right?"

"Whatever," Sydney finally said, emotionless. "It was an accident. You're prone to those, right?"

"*So* prone!" I nodded vigorously. "My mom even says *I* was an accident!"

Would it surprise you that no one laughed?

Sydney looked from Hailey to Lucy and the rest of the girls. "I think it would be fun to have Lizbeth around. We don't laugh enough."

"Oh, we don't laugh at all," Lucy said, smiling brightly. Sydney rolled her eyes at her.

Hailey sighed. "Welcome to our lunch group, then."

I glanced over at Tess, who just shrugged and bit the end off a carrot with gusto. That girl had an unsettling relationship with vegetables.

"Hailey wants us to be friends," Sydney quietly said to me. "She doesn't like drama. We need to get along."

"For her sake?"

Her expression was deadly serious. "For ours."

CHAPTER 11

Sydney peeked at the plastic-wrapped item on her lunch tray, then looked at Hailey. I'd noticed that if Hailey decided not to eat whatever was on her lunch tray, no one else did either.

Thankfully, today was PB&J day, and that passed inspection. Hailey pinched a bite-sized piece off her sandwich and popped it in her mouth. Leaning forward, she caught my eye. "Is your group really doing *art* for the talent show?" Something behind her eyes seemed to be moving, calculating odds.

"Yes," I said with as much dignity as I could muster. "Real art. Which is the hardest thing to do."

Several girls pressed their lips together as if they wanted to giggle but were afraid to.

Hailey opened her milk and took a drink. "My

group always wins first place in the talent show, did you know that?"

Tess was straining to overhear our conversation. Joseph seemed distracted, though. He kept making fists, then relaxing his hands and shaking them out. He reminded me of a boxer before a big match.

"Are we going to win this year, Sydney?" Hailey's voice was calm and low.

"I told you, we have a great routine." Sydney looked around at the girls, smirking. "And once we get Ms. Mayweather's permission to rehearse in the music room after school, there's no way your 'art'"—here she used air quotes—"is going to beat a real act with dancing and singing."

Amid the din of chatter and trays hitting the tables and sneakers shuffling across the floor, an eerie silence had descended upon our end of the table. A threat hung in the air.

In a flash, I understood. Sydney had to earn her place in this group, just like me, over and over. The talent show was her next test. My stomach felt a little queasy, reminding me how I had felt leading up to my report on supernovas. Needing to score points to win a friendship isn't a pleasant experience.

On the way back to class, Tess cut in line to get behind me. "Why didn't you sit with us? We're your friends."

I turned around, and she bumped into me, causing a chain reaction down the line. "I know that! But maybe I want to be friends with other people, too."

"You can be friendly with those girls, but you can't be friends," Tess replied, her voice matter-of-fact.

I nervously pressed down on the curling corners of my name tag. "So . . . does that mean you're mad at me?"

She shook her head. "We feel bad for you when you sit with them, but we don't get mad. We want you to be happy."

"Well, so do they," I said, sounding defensive.

"No," Tess said. "They want you to make them happy."

I couldn't help feeling she was right. It was amazing how much the Weirdos knew about friendship, because no one wanted to be friends with them.

Today our class had "study skills" after lunch, which basically meant we were supposed to sit in the media center and stay out of trouble for an hour. As we filed in, Tess whispered to me, "Joseph and I are skipping study hall to work on a project, okay?"

Joseph appeared next to us. "We can't tell you about the project because it's a secret."

"Joseph, that's the definition of a secret," Tess said, glaring at him. "Lizbeth, if anyone asks, tell them we definitely stayed in the media center."

"Paul said to meet him in the art room," Joseph said. "No one will be there this hour."

"Joseph!" Tess snapped.

Of course, I waited for a few minutes and then followed them. As I got closer to the art room, I heard scuffling, like desks or chairs scraping across the floor, then a loud thud.

"You're going to get yourself killed," Paul said. "Take another swing at me, man. But this time don't jump back and cover your face!"

I lurched into the classroom just as Joseph swung at Paul, who easily dodged the blow. Tess sat at Mr. Westchester's desk, doodling on a sketch pad.

"Stop!" I yelled. "Joseph, what are you doing? You can't beat up Paul!"

"This is none of your business." Joseph wiped at his eyes, as if trying not to cry. "Paul, next I will try the head-butt. Brace yourself." He rushed straight at Paul, head-butting him in the stomach. He bounced off like a rubber ball.

"You can't *announce* your next move, Joseph," Paul said. "Plan it, but don't say it!"

"I didn't want to hurt you!" Joseph rubbed the top of his head.

"That's the whole point of fighting!" Paul snapped, his brows knotting. "We're not leaving this room until you prove you can hurt me!"

"Why are you guys fighting?" I demanded.

"Shh!" Tess hissed at me. "Keep your voice down or someone will—"

Mr. Westchester walked into the classroom. He had crumbs at the corners of his mouth, a half-eaten sandwich in one hand and a Coke in the other. For a moment we all stood frozen, including him.

"There'd better be a very good explanation for this," Mr. Westchester said finally. "Because the one thing I will never tolerate—and I can tolerate a lot— is violence."

Joseph looked at Paul, who was studying his shoes. Finally, Joseph sighed and his shoulders slumped forward. "Paul is teaching me how to fight."

"Someone steals his lunch every day," I offered.

"How did you—never mind," Joseph said, gritting his teeth.

"That's why you want to learn how to fight?" Mr. Westchester asked, sitting on the edge of his desk. "Someone's bullying you?"

"No," Joseph said quickly.

"If you're being bullied, you can tell me," Mr. Westchester said. "I can help."

Joseph looked thoroughly unconvinced.

"There's a group of boys," Paul said. "Some of them have older brothers who hang out near here after school. They *wish* they could bully Joseph. But since Joseph and I are friends, they usually keep their distance."

Mr. Westchester nodded thoughtfully and bit into his sandwich. He seemed relieved that Joseph wasn't in immediate danger.

I didn't think that was quite true, though. I had seen his bloody nose the other day. I glanced at Tess, wondering if she was going to say anything, but she turned away. I figured she was mad I had gotten their little fight club busted, even though they were already making plenty of noise before I showed up.

"Joseph wants to learn to defend himself so that he doesn't feel like he's only safe when I'm around,"

Paul said. "It's a mental thing, you know? If he was confident, he'd walk different, act different . . . . Maybe they would decide he wasn't worth the risk."

After a few more seconds of thoughtful chewing, Mr. Westchester swallowed his sandwich bite and said, "So you think it's important to defend yourself?"

"The world is filled with mean people," Tess said matter-of-factly. "You have to be ready."

"True." Mr. Westchester took a sip of his Coke. "But defending yourself with your fists is not the answer. Because then, nothing will change. The real weapon is your brain. With your brain, you don't have to run from a broken world. You can fix it."

"I can't fix it if I'm in the hospital," Joseph muttered.

"Which is why I think getting some adults involved is—"

Joseph cut him off. "All I need is one chance to stand up to them, to prove to them that I'm not the weak loser they think I am."

"Joseph, you are not a weak loser," Mr. Westchester said solemnly. "And you don't need to prove that to anyone. If those boys bother you again, promise me you'll tell me or another teacher, instead of trying to confront them yourself."

Joseph looked down and nodded, though it wasn't exactly the most convincing nod I'd ever seen. Paul crossed his arms, which I suspected was his way of holding his thoughts close. Tess glanced at me and I accidentally smiled. She smiled back. It was hard to stay at odds with Tess.

"Meanwhile, we're facing a different fight." Mr. Westchester shooed Tess out of his chair and sat down. "With the district running out of money, Ms. Camp needs our help to save our arts program." He swung his legs onto the desk, crossing them at the ankles. "When we're done with this talent show, the school board members are going to ask themselves how they could have ever considered getting rid of it."

Paul's eyes narrowed. "Don't get your hopes up. The school board won't keep the program unless they have enough money for it. And the only parents who have enough money to make a difference don't care about this school. They don't even want their kids going here. They're just waiting for a spot at a better school to open up. This fundraiser isn't going to change anything."

"Hmm." Mr. Westchester finished off his Coke and stared pensively at the empty can, tapping on the metal with a fingertip. "You know what hurts most when you're an adult? It's not the times you were knocked down. It's the times you didn't even get in the ring."

The room was silent. Great delivery but the line fell flat. He didn't know his audience all that well yet. No one here was a boxer.

After a moment, though, Tess raised her hand. "Mr. Westchester? I have a plan."

CHAPTER 12

After school the next day, Tess stood at the door to Mr. Westchester's classroom. She had told us we would need to stay late today, but otherwise she'd kept us largely in suspense about the details of her plan. Given the extremes of her wardrobe, I was ready for anything.

"Welcome to the first-ever meeting of the Art Club for Undeserved Students with Exceptionally Incredible Futures!"

"Did you mean *under-served*?" I asked, pausing in the doorway. "Like, the kids in this school are under-served?"

"Oooo." Tess's face brightened. "That sounds better."

I set my book bag down, wary of Tess's enthusiasm, in case it was contagious. Joseph was already sitting at a table, watching some superhero action movie on his phone. The loud smacks and screams told me it wasn't going well for someone. He glanced up, then seeing it was just me, shifted his phone so I wouldn't be in his line of sight.

He was still mad about me barging in on yesterday's fight club, I figured. To be fair, I hadn't known if his fight with Paul was real or fake at first. I thought I deserved bonus points for trying to save his life.

Paul was reading, earbuds in, hair falling forward so I couldn't see much of his expression.

"Let's add your suggestion to the list," Tess said, grabbing me by the hand and leading me to another table.

"What suggestion?"

"Your suggestion for the name of the club, silly."

"Can't we just call it Art Club?"

She bit the end of a marker as she studied her list of titles. "Hmm. Maybe . . . Art Club Society for Exceptional Beings." She wrote this down and looked up for my reaction.

I pulled out a chair and sat down. "How does this qualify as a plan? What does an art club even do?"

"It *raises awareness*," she said, as if this should be

obvious. "If we start an official group, that'll show the school board and all the other adults in charge of these decisions that Plains Creek students really care about the arts. And the more attention we get for the art club and the talent show, the easier it will be to raise money to keep the arts programs running."

"Okay . . . but speaking of the talent show, don't we still need to pick an art project?"

Tess spun on her heel and walked behind Mr. Westchester's desk. "I'm getting to that. It's Step Four of the plan."

She held up a sheet of lined paper covered with neat handwriting. Tess's plans, I must admit, are a thing of beauty. "We'll start by making posters and drafting an ad for the morning announcements to tell students about the club. *Then* we'll work with Mr. Westchester to choose our art projects for the show."

I looked around the room. "Where is he, by the way?"

"He ran to the teachers' lounge a second ago. He's buying us soft drinks and candy."

My mood improved. "Have you ever googled him? I think he's famous. At least famous in the art world."

"For real? So . . . why is he working here?"

"Good question."

"Sugar water and empty carbs coming through!" Mr. Westchester walked in, arms loaded down.

Tess gave him the sign of SuperChicken.

"I hope that means thank you in your language," said Mr. Westchester dryly.

"It means *we're a team*," said Tess. Then she exchanged a look with me. How had Mr. Westchester ended up on our team? We wanted to know more. What catastrophe could possibly have driven a successful artist to seek refuge here with sixth-graders in the bowels of a falling-apart middle school? My breathing became shallow just imagining it.

Suddenly Tess threw a marker at Joseph. He ducked to one side and it sailed past. "Turn that off! It's time for Art Club!"

"I'm learning some new moves here," he snapped. "Leave me alone."

"Not until you help make posters!"

Tess had assigned each of us a task that capitalized on our talents. She had also nailed down the logistics we would need to share with potential Art Club members.

The time: an hour after school every Tuesday

and Thursday. (When I asked about Wednesdays, I was promptly shushed.)

The place: The art room, under Mr. Westchester's supervision.

The perks: art supplies and snacks provided.

Paul was supposed to come up with catchy messages for the posters. He'd already decided each grade should have a different campaign pitch. The sixth-graders would want an easy way to make friends. The seventh-graders would want more art experience before picking elective classes in eighth grade. And the eighth-graders would want to do as much art as possible before high school, when electives are harder to grab.

Joseph did the hand lettering. My job was to apply glue, glitter, and paint to the posters.

Meanwhile, Tess worked with Mr. Westchester to draft the school-wide announcement and then a press release for the local newspaper. Mr. Westchester had to explain to Tess how newspapers even work: Reporters are assigned to different topics, so her first job was to find the right reporter who would be interested in school-related news.

When I got to the last poster in the stack, Joseph handed me the one he had spent extra time on. Paul read it before I did and just shook his head, so it was clear that Joseph had come up with the message himself.

Join Art Club
Because the Other Clubs Are Full

I rolled my eyes and began applying glue along the edges of the paper. Tess was going to unleash her wrath on him when she spied this one in the hallway.

Mr. Westchester sat on the edge of his desk, eating snacks, while Tess was busy working on his laptop. Finally, he said, "Ready to talk about the talent show project?"

He seemed to be addressing the four of us as a unit.

Paul pointed to Tess. "You got us into this."

Tess nodded. "I know." Closing the laptop, she flopped her hands open. "So far, the talent show has garage bands, singing, a magic act, skits, dance routines, and I heard that the Thompson twins are doing synchronized armpit farts to Beethoven's Fifth Symphony. There's no way we're beating that."

Mr. Westchester stifled a laugh. "I thought you were artists."

"We are." Tess spoke for the group.

"Then let the crowd have their armpit farts. No harm done. You can still make art, you know. It all coexists in the real world anyway." He paused while we considered this. "You want my help picking a project?"

We nodded.

"Deal. Since we have limited supplies to work with, I'd suggest drawings or paintings. Paint is more colorful and eye-catching than charcoal or pencil, so for a talent show setting, paintings are probably the better bet. As for what *kind* of paintings you'll do, that's subject to more discussion. They should all share a similar approach or theme, since you'll present them together. But there's still time to figure that out. Now go put out your posters and head home. I'll see you in class tomorrow, and we'll get to work then."

Walking out the door after our first-ever Art Club meeting, I noticed something strange. I felt lighter. Happier. My stomach wasn't in knots.

I didn't even care that my stupid name tag curled up at the edges and was smudged.

Later that night, I collapsed on the sofa with a bag of store-brand Oreos. The name-brand cookies were better, but Mom wouldn't take me grocery shopping with her after the Claire incident, so I'd lost any control over our purchases.

Thanks to a hot shower and clean fleece jammies, all was right with my world. Except for the parts that weren't, and I was too exhausted to solve those problems right now. The doorbell rang but Mom was busy cleaning the kitchen, so I got up to answer it.

"Darien!" I swung the door open wide. "Mom! One of the movers is here!"

Darien stuck out his hand and we did our secret handshake.

Mom came around the corner from the kitchen, wiping her hands on a dishtowel. "Darien! How good to see you again. Come in."

"No, thank you, Ms. Murphy. Have to get to class. I just wanted to bring this by." He held out a cardboard box. "We found it in the moving van. We must have missed it when we unloaded."

I reached for the box, which wasn't especially heavy. "What is it?"

"I didn't look inside."

Mom opened the box as I held it steady. "Family photos!" she gasped. "Oh, Darien! Thank you! I didn't even realize they had gone missing. I'm not done unpacking yet. If these had been lost . . . well, thank you."

"No worries. Glad to help," he said, then smiled at me. "How's the new school, Lizbeth?"

I hesitated. This was a loaded question.

"Lizbeth has discovered her inner artist," Mom blabbed. "She's started an art club, and she's working on an art project that's going to be featured at her school's talent show!"

"Wow!" Darien put a hand over his heart as if the news was truly staggering. Maybe it would have been, if any of what Mom had just said were true.

"The show's two weeks from this Friday night, and it's open to the public," Mom went on.

"That's great," said Darien. "My sister will be in town then. Maybe we'll swing by."

I smiled weakly, deciding it was best not to mention that I didn't have anything to display yet.

After Darien left, Mom set the box of family photos on the couch and returned to the kitchen, working on a new recipe for dinner. She had been trying new recipes every night, watching videos, looking up tips and hints online.

I had been trying not to spend as much time online, seeing as how the internet had ruined my life in multiple ways. If I ever saw Eva and Camden again, they would probably need to look at my name tag to remember who I was.

Pulling a photo album from the box, I settled onto the couch. The cover was fake brown leather with gold letters: *Family is Forever*. I drifted back to when my mom had bought it at the craft store while Dad had wandered the aisles looking for cosplay supplies. A cold pebble dropped into my stomach, another reminder of the divorce.

As I flipped through the pages, though, I couldn't help but smile and even chuckle. Photos were memories and we had some great ones. Dad and I were Wonder Woman and Superman for our first con. Wonder Woman is the gateway cosplay for countless little girls. Once you taste the power of those laser bracelets, and realize fashion accessories can tie an outfit together *and* destroy an enemy base, you're hooked.

The last page of the album was of our last Christmas together as a family before Dad left. My stomach felt cold again. I ran my finger down the page, snagging a nail on the binding ring in the center. The ring stuck out really far, with plenty of room for more photos.

Adding a new page, or a new family member, would be so easy and painless as far as this album was concerned. Maybe this explained how my parents had gotten their stupid ideas about divorce and dating and fresh starts. Perhaps craft stores, with their insistence that you could always expand a project or start a new one, had caused the downfall of the nuclear family.

I lifted the book to toss it back in the box when an old photo fell out. It was square, with a white border around the bent and torn edges.

"Mom?" I called. "Who's this?" In the picture, two little boys wore Halloween costumes, dressed up as Batman and Robin. They carried plastic pumpkins that brimmed with candy.

Mom came out from the kitchen and sat next to me. She rested the fingers of one hand against her lips as she took the picture from me with the other. "It's your dad. And his little brother."

"Brother?" I didn't know Dad had a brother. I had an uncle I'd never met!

"He died when your father was ten," Mom said softly. "They were riding bikes. A car swerved and hit his brother, killing him instantly. It was a hit-and-run. No one heard your dad yelling for help. And this was before everybody had a cell phone. Their mom, your grandmom, went looking for them when they didn't come home for dinner."

I touched the picture gently. "Why didn't he ever tell me?"

"He's never learned how to talk about it." Mom's voice trembled slightly. "I think he's afraid to, because it hurts so much."

I thought about supernovas—explosions so powerful that they create black holes, patches of emptiness that suck in everything around them. I wiped my cheek, where a tear had rolled down. "There's a big hole in his heart."

She wiped her cheeks too and then kissed the top of my head. "There are holes in everyone's heart, honey. I'm sorry that your dad hasn't been able to share his with you. I think some part of him is still out there, in the dark."

I knew, in theory, that my parents were real people, who'd had their own lives before I showed up. I'd even seen their birth certificates. My dad had once weighed nine pounds, five ounces. I could have carried him around in my backpack! Except for that being weird and probably illegal.

It was shocking to realize that Dad had been holding such a big, painful secret inside for so long, and I'd had no idea. What other secrets did he have that I'd never known about? I hated the idea that he'd been walking around with a big empty space inside and he'd never been able to talk about it. Was that what he'd meant when he'd said, *I gave up on me?*

I wished I knew how to fill a hole like that.

CHAPTER 13

The Friday morning announcements blared into the classroom. Ms. Farris winced and ducked, as if this was the start of an air raid. Tess folded her hands, beaming. Joseph nudged her and wiggled his eyebrows in excitement.

"Attention students! Mr. Westchester is now offering Art Club every Tuesday and Thursday after school. Join us and explore the wonder of making art on a doomed planet. Contact the club founders—Lizbeth, Joseph, Paul, or Tess, in Ms. Farris's homeroom—for more information. And be sure to attend the talent show, where stunning original works by the founding members will be on display. This will be a night for the history books! Please, no flash photography."

I slumped down in my seat in mortification.

Sydney and Hailey whispered back and forth, and soon the entire room was buzzing. Tess was floating on her own personal cloud of bliss.

"I wish you'd shown us the announcement before you submitted it," I muttered to her. "I would've had some edits for you."

"What's wrong with it?" Tess asked defensively.

"It's a little . . . over-the-top."

"That's. The. Point," she said, pausing slightly between each word for emphasis. "We'll get more interest this way!"

I shook my head. She made such huge plans without thinking through how they would impact the rest of us. It reminded me of someone, though I couldn't put my finger on who.

On the way to lunch a couple of hours later, Joseph whispered, slightly in awe, "Hailey's friends seem kind of mad. But all the other kids want Art Club to win the talent show!"

"Get used to it. Heavy is the head that wears the crown," Tess said, hardly paying attention to him. She was quoting Shakespeare! His dramas inspired a lot of anime plots. If I weren't so frustrated with her, I'd be impressed.

"Wearing the crown seems a little premature,

don't you think?" I asked. "We don't even know what we're doing yet!"

"Well, whatever we do, we have to win." She lifted her head, her chin trembling. "My dad is coming to the show. I need him to see that I can still be the daughter he wants, the one who doesn't dream about superhero chickens. The one who is normal and pretty and all that stupid stuff."

Paul leaned toward her. "Have you ever asked him if he wants a normal, pretty, stupid daughter?"

"Everyone wants a stupid daughter, Paul!" Tess snapped.

A teacher shook her finger at us in warning for talking in the halls. We lowered our heads as we passed her.

I swallowed, trying to think of some encouraging words for Tess, since encouragement was reportedly what real friends were supposed to do. But really—wasn't she right, just a little? Not about being stupid, of course, but adults always tell us we're supposed to stand out. Until we do. Then they yell at us to get back in line, to smooth down our hair, to quit acting up. My mom once told me that most parents spend the first two years of a baby's life cheering for the baby to walk and talk, then the next sixteen begging the kid to sit down and shut up.

"Let's focus on figuring out what kind of paintings we're going to do," Paul said matter-of-factly. "We're running out of time. And if we're going to win, it had better be good." He winked at Tess, but she didn't seem to notice. Then he stopped at the cafeteria door to let us go on without him.

Hailey filed past, watching us out of the corner of her eye.

Mom set out three plates for dinner that night.

"Dad's coming?" I squealed.

"So he says," Mom replied. I squealed again as she lit an apple-cinnamon-scented candle on the fireplace mantle. It was almost like old times.

The doorbell rang and I rushed to answer it. My hand was on the knob before I considered that Dad had tricked me before. Rushing back to the kitchen, I grabbed the Lysol from under the sink and ran back to the door.

"What are you doing?" Mom called after me. "Answer the door!"

I cracked open the door and thrust the can out first, ready to defend my home.

Dad was alone. He gently pushed open the door, then stepped inside and wrapped me up in a bear hug. I hugged back.

"Lysol?" he said, taking the can from me and setting it aside. "Seriously? Where's your mom?"

"In here," Mom called from the kitchen. Dad went in to say hello. Seeing each other, they paused. They used to hug or kiss when they saw each other at the end of the day. Even after two years, I still found myself hoping they would be normal with each other again. But they didn't seem to remember what our normal was.

I panicked. Sometimes when they froze like that, the next thing they said was bad.

"Let me show you my temporary bedroom," I chirped, taking Dad's hand.

Moments later he stepped slowly over the threshold, looking at the bare walls and the unmade bed.

"I was neater at home," I said, embarrassed. I nudged a sock under the bed with my foot.

Dad frowned. "You always had a place for everything and everything in its place."

"They took my room apart, Dad." My jaw got

tight and my lips puckered into an angry circle. "I lost all my places."

He waved his hand around. "You have new places."

Stifling a groan, I pressed my palms to my face. Suddenly, yet again, I was trying to make him understand me and he was blaming me for being misunderstood.

"Your blinds are down," he said.

"Yes, because I hate the view from here." I fought to keep my voice steady. "Can we go back to our old house? All of us? I could go back to my old school. I never got in trouble there. Everyone liked me and I had a million friends. And my room was always neat."

He looked at me so sadly that for a second I thought he might actually agree. Instead he said, "Mom told me what happened at the store."

"Don't change the subject."

"I'm not. Tonight, you are the subject. Mom and I are concerned about you, peaches."

So they weren't having dinner because they wanted to see each other. They were having dinner because they thought I was the problem. How could all of us look at the same picture but see such different things?

I crossed my arms defiantly. "I'm only looking

out for your best interests, Dad. Claire isn't good enough for you."

"This isn't just about Claire. I know you heard Mom and me arguing the other day, and I'm sorry about that. I did want to talk to you about seeing a counselor, but not because I'm mad at Mom."

"Are you going to see the counselor with her, or just with me?"

"Just you. It's way too late to fix our marriage. But I do need to work on being a better dad. And Mom thinks you might have questions about"—he paused and took a deep breath—"my brother. And there are so many things we can talk about."

I felt like someone had tied sandbags to my heart.

Mom called us down to dinner. Dad's face brightened. "I'm starving. Your mom made my favorite casserole, didn't she?"

At least his stomach remembered where he belonged.

After dinner, Mom insisted on clearing the dishes by herself. Dad asked to see my room again.

I trudged up the stairs behind him, frustrated.

Dinner had been a waste of time. Both my parents had been polite and pleasant. Dad and Claire hadn't broken up yet. Mom was still going to have coffee with some dumb guy next week. But no one acted like the world was ending.

The thought of someday having to eliminate Mom's boyfriends, pick them off one by one, exhausted me. I would never admit it, but I was tired of fighting.

Dad walked into my room and lifted my blinds halfway. He sat on the bed and leaned against the window. "Tell me more about your science project."

"It was just supernovas." I nudged the carpet with my toe as I lingered in the doorway.

Dad patted the bed next to him. "Tell me about supernovas, then."

Dragging my feet, I meandered over to the bed and flopped down, careful not to look out the window. "I know what you're doing," I said. "You're trying to make this lousy place feel like home."

He grabbed my hand in his. "Look up, Lizbeth. Please."

I glanced up at the stars, then turned away, my eyes stinging. Mom had cleaned the window. The night sky sparkled.

Dad still held my hand. "I know I ruined things with us, with you and your mom. But we can still be a family—a different kind of family than we were before. And you are still you. I've always loved that you have such a strong sense of who you are as a person, that you're never afraid to be yourself—"

"But I am!" I choked out. "I'm not even sure who myself *is* now! This new life doesn't feel like mine. Everything that I used to count on is gone. My old friends, my old house—even the toilet is in a different place here. Nothing is where it's supposed to be, including you."

"Hey, peaches. Look out there."

I looked, tears threatening to fall.

"On the darkest nights, sailors can find their way home by starlight. Even without a compass, without a radio, the stars will always guide them home. When you steer by the stars, you can never be lost."

I leaned my head against his chest. "Dad, you're missing the point. You and Mom were my home. You were my pin on the map. But that pin is gone. Where will the stars take me now?"

"To a new kind of home," he said. "I don't know what that looks like exactly, and neither does your mom, but it's real. It's out there. And it's waiting for all of us. All the Universe needs from you is a little trust."

Did I believe him? I didn't know. The important thing was that he was trying. So I let him hold me and together we looked up at the stars until it was time for him to go.

During art class with the rest of Ms. Farris's homeroom, Mr. Westchester was still giving us small exercises to do each day—nothing impressive enough to enter in the talent show. But he let Tess use his laptop when she finished with the class activities, and I could tell she was formulating a plan. I liked her more every day.

On Tuesday, I walked to Art Club with my podmates as if this had always been our routine. Nobody else was there, so apparently our posters and Tess's announcement hadn't inspired our fellow students to join. I deflated a little, not relishing the idea of the four of us alone onstage at the talent show, with everyone else staring.

Looking at his phone, Mr. Westchester flashed the sign of SuperChicken. "I did as you requested."

Tess returned the signal. "Excellent." She walked over toward a stash of painting supplies, all new, still wrapped in plastic. There were even four slightly rickety-looking easels stacked against the wall. In my experience, you can talk an adult out of anything . . . until they spend money. So, now it was official: I was painting some kind of picture and entering it in the talent show.

"Also," said Tess, "I emailed the local arts reporter at the newspaper, suggesting a story on Art Club, and she responded! She says she's in! She's going to make sure our press release about the talent show runs in the paper, and she's going to come see the show and interview all of us then!" Tess beamed and clapped like a seal. "I told her that Art Club is led by a world-famous failed artist, Mr. Westchester. I told her it's changing lives!"

"I'm not a failed artist!" Mr. Westchester protested. "And—hold on, how did you even know—" Then he glared at me.

"I only told one person," I said. "Just Tess. She wanted to know your origin story. Trust me, the truth was better than anything she would make up. I was doing you a favor."

"But we still don't get how you ended up here,"

Tess added. "Did you experience a horrible, public failure?"

"That's not important," Mr. Westchester snapped. "Art Club isn't about me. It's about the four of you creating—well, you haven't even decided what exactly you'll be creating, have you? How about you concentrate on that, instead of my sordid past?"

"Isn't it obvious?" Tess practically shouted. "Self-portraits! That's what we'll do." She flailed an unopened package of paint brushes in the air for emphasis. "I'll be on stage, next to my self-portrait. The newspaper reporter will be snapping pictures, asking soul-searching questions about me . . . and my dad will be there to see the whole thing."

"Tess," I said, trying to keep my voice reasonable, "everything I've expressed about myself so far at this school has been a disaster. I don't want to put it on display for the whole world to laugh at."

"I don't think you understand what a self-portrait is," she replied. "A self-portrait is the most intimate work an artist can create, a window into her soul."

"Exactly!" I snapped.

Mr. Westchester sat at his desk, his head swiveling between us like he was at a tennis match.

I held out my hands, palms up, surrendering to the inevitability that was Tess.

"Now, I have a bunch of famous self-portraits queued up on Mr. Westchester's laptop to show us." She looked at him. "If you want to go to the teacher's lounge, this will keep us occupied for about twenty minutes."

"Nah," he said, shrugging. "Might as well stick around in case you have any questions."

She turned off the lights as Mr. Westchester projected his screen onto the whiteboard. He sat with us at our table, facing the board.

Images scrolled past, one after another. I could feel the cool air blowing from the vents and hear the soft sounds of our breath. My shoulders relaxed as I began to breathe deeply. The hum of a computer in a dark room was hypnotic.

It felt like we were at an aquarium, watching colorful fish swim by, each one pausing for an inspection. Some self-portraits had dark colors and heavily drawn, wavy lines. They looked like images resting on the bottom of the ocean inside a forgotten shipwreck. Images that should have been screams but seemed more like echoes now. I felt sad for the artists. Had they been heard when they were still alive?

Other pictures were wild and bright. The colors and lines danced right off the page. If you stared too long at them, your feet would wiggle in their shoes and you'd feel breathless. Many of these artists had done more than one self-portrait, which made complete sense. Some people never run out of things to tell you about themselves.

Every once in a while, a totally bizarre one floated by and we'd all laugh aloud. I didn't think those artists would have been offended at our laughing. The weirdest self-portraits also seemed to be the most matter-of-fact ones, totally free from self-doubt and judgment.

The show over, Mr. Westchester returned to his desk and sat facing us. "Seeing all those, what did you learn?"

"I would never paint a self-portrait like those," Joseph said. "None of the guys painted themselves looking like they lifted anything heavier than a paintbrush. Why make yourself look weak? If you get to decide how your self-portrait looks, make yourself look like an action hero."

"But then it wouldn't be a real self-portrait," I said. "It would be a fantasy."

Joseph shot me a dirty look.

"I didn't mean it as an insult!" I protested. "I just meant—I'm guessing a self-portrait shouldn't be about how you want other people to see you, it should be about how you see yourself."

Tess leaned toward Joseph. "You're awesome just the way you are."

He looked away.

Mr. Westchester hopped up from his desk. "Actually, Lizbeth and Joseph, you're both right. The purpose of a self-portrait is to reveal the truth. But it doesn't have to be the literal truth. It's not about looks or how accurately you draw an exact physical reality. It's how you see yourself."

Joseph threw his hands in the air. "How I see myself is my whole entire problem."

Paul's eyes narrowed, but not in a mean way. It was as if he heard something in Joseph's words, something new, something that caught his imagination.

"Look," Mr. Westchester continued, "you can do this. Play around with ideas. You know how to take a selfie, right? And you know how to use filters and retouching apps. Doing a self-portrait isn't so different. We'll be working with our hands instead of our phones, that's all. The result may not match exactly how you look in real life, but then, neither do your selfies. The point is to express something about yourself that feels true."

We all absorbed this in silence for a moment.

"You know what?" Mr. W said. "You're going to put your work in the shredder before you leave. Right now, I want you to focus on writing down ideas, thoughts, shapes—whatever comes to mind. Remember, no one will see this."

"Wait," Tess said. "Why do we have to shred our work?"

"Because I want you to make it safe for your imagination to come out and play. I don't want any pressure on you. Except for one thing."

We all leaned forward. He grabbed his phone and tapped it a few times, then turned it to face us. "When I start this timer, you will have fifteen minutes to work. You may not pause. Even if all you do is make squiggly marks, keep going, no matter what."

We scrambled to get ready, grabbing paper and pencils.

He held his finger above the *start* button. "Listen to the voice that matters most, for a change. And tell the truth. Whatever it looks like to you."

And we started.

CHAPTER 14

I found out there was a reason Tess didn't want to have Art Club on Wednesdays. Wednesday was Taco Night at Paul's.

"Explain Taco Night to me again," Mom murmured, squinting at mailboxes and porches as she drove slowly down Paul's street, looking for the right house number. The streetlight had burned out, making this a challenging task.

"Paul's mom works a double shift on Wednesdays, so she makes a big batch of taco meat on Tuesday for Wednesday's dinner. She won't be there, but his dad is. Paul makes rice and beans, Tess makes queso, and Joseph makes Snickers chimichangas. They do homework after dinner."

I didn't mention that after dinner Tess and Joseph would also unveil the latest chapter of SuperChicken.

Explaining SuperChicken would require her full attention and more time than we had.

"What on Earth is a Snickers chimichanga?"

"I can't wait to find out."

"Glad you're bringing your lactase pills." She stopped in front of the house with the right numbers. I'd thought our new house was small, but Paul's was *tiny*. I was pretty sure I had seen larger storage lockers on TV shows.

Before I got out of the car, I asked, "Are you going to have coffee with that guy from work?"

"No," she sighed. "I was supposed to, but I canceled. I think you need more time to adjust to the move. I want to find a counselor who can help us navigate all these changes before I bring someone new into our lives."

"For his own safety," I said, voicing her unspoken concern.

"Exactly," she chuckled.

She was laughing, but I didn't think either one of us felt happy. I didn't understand it. Mom loved making me happy. It was her default setting. She couldn't help herself. When we watched TV, she let me pick the shows. When we made cookies, she ate the ones with the burned edges. But making me happy wasn't making her happy anymore. In fact, it might even be making her sad.

She walked me to the door, and Paul answered. His dad waved from his recliner and called out a hello. I glanced around as Mom double-checked what time she was supposed to pick me up.

Paul's home was nothing like mine. His was bursting with color: pictures on the walls, fruit-bowls on tables, books stacked high everywhere, some resting with their pages open. Classical music filtered in from the kitchen.

After Mom left, Paul said, "You can leave your shoes here," and hooked his thumb toward to a pile of footwear by the door.

From the kitchen, Joseph called, "His mom says shoes carry way more bacteria than toilet seats! And she's a nurse, so she should know."

"She sounds very wise," I said. She sounded almost as great as my mom.

"Lizbeth!" Tess squealed when Paul led me into the kitchen. She was stirring a bowl of queso with one hand as she shook a jar of pickled jalapeños into it with the other. She firmly believed in the transfor-mative power of the pickling process.

"Welcome to Taco Night!" said Joseph. He was

unwrapping big Snickers bars and dropping them into a bowl next to a package of flour tortillas.

"Want something to drink?" Paul asked me. "We have water."

"Water's great," I said, taking my lactase pills out of my pocket. I had to prepare; this wasn't dinner. This was an intestinal depth charge.

It only took the four of us about twenty minutes to get dinner ready. Paul asked me to set the kitchen table while he put food on a tray and carried it out to his dad, who was still sitting in the recliner in the living room.

"Want me to cue up a movie, Pops?" Paul asked. His dad said something quietly and they held hands. Before I could look away in embarrassment, Joseph grabbed my right hand and Tess grabbed my left one. Everyone bowed their heads as Paul sang.

Because we have food in a world of hunger
And hope in a time of fear
And friends who share our journey,
We give thanks as we draw near.

The hush that followed the last note lingered. We let it float through the air, invisible, willing it to stay. His voice was unmistakably mesmerizing.

Paul was the one I had heard singing in the halls

at school, not the janitor. Why hadn't he wanted me to know it was him? He should be singing at the talent show—or on TV.

"Rub-a-dub-dub, thanks for the grub!" Joseph said, lifting the lid off the pot of taco meat and releasing a steam cloud. On cue, we all leaned in to inhale, then groaned in happiness.

"My mom is a great cook," Paul said. The feeding frenzy commenced. I had to carefully time when to reach for toppings to avoid getting stabbed by a flying fork or Joseph's lightning-fast fists of fury reaching for more meat. If his mortal enemy had been a taco, it would have been soundly defeated by now.

"She taught us to cook, too," Joseph said, lettuce falling out of the corners of his mouth. "You have to come in the summer for cooking lessons, though."

"Awesome," I said between bites. "I can't believe you do this every Wednesday."

"Correction," Tess said, fishing in the queso bowl with a spoon and scooping up extra servings of jalapeños onto her plate. "*We* do this every Wednesday."

I felt suddenly warm inside, and not just from the pickled jalapeños.

After dinner, we cleaned up, then headed to the basement to do homework and go over the newest chapter of SuperChicken. On the way down, Paul picked up a baby monitor. Surprised, I looked around for signs of a baby in the house.

Tess took my hand, gently guiding me down the stairs. After a few minutes I realized Paul was using the monitor to listen for his dad. In case his dad needed anything. His dad hadn't gotten out of the recliner since I had arrived. Slowly, I realized he probably couldn't, not without Paul's help.

Taco Night wasn't just about eating great food. It was about keeping Paul company while he took care of his own father.

Mom had told me there are holes in everyone's heart. I was starting to see that she was right.

CHAPTER 15

When I walked up to the school entrance on Thursday morning, my breath puffed out as mist. I paused, exhaling hard, watching the cloud form and disappear. Smushing down my name tag, which refused to stay securely affixed to my shirt because the adhesive was worn out, I looked at the kids around me. Everyone exhaled in white puffs as they walked into the building, as if we had been asked to extinguish the little fires we carried inside. Summer was flip-flops and freedom, but fall had magic tricks.

After getting my books out of my locker, I slammed it closed, only to see Hailey standing right there. Lucy was beside her.

Hailey's eyes glittered. Lucy bolted for the classroom, then turned and mouthed "sorry" to me.

"Hi," I said to Hailey. We were friends. I had earned my spot, right?

"You need to back off on this talent show, Lizbeth."

"I—what?"

"A press release? Seriously? My mom saw it on the website for the paper. It's ridiculous."

Considering the tone of Tess's school announcement, I suspected that *ridiculous* was an accurate way to describe her press release for the newspaper. But I chose a diplomatic response: "All publicity is good publicity, right?" Some of my cosplay friends liked to say this when group photos caught them at unflattering angles.

Hailey tapped the toe of her shoe against the linoleum tiles, and then traced around a little smudge mark. "You need to stop making the rest of us look bad. Or I'll make sure that you look bad."

"But the talent show is to save the arts program. It's not even about us."

"Keep it that way." Hailey's expression was cold. "You don't get to be the new kid who started an art club and became the school hero. You are a weirdo. That's who you are and that's who you're going to stay."

I stared at her, gasping like a fish. "I didn't . . ." But I stopped there. If I told her that starting Art Club was Tess's idea, then Tess would be her next target. I couldn't do that to my friend—my real friend. "You can win, I don't care about that. I just want to help the school raise money. We can't raise money if people don't hear about the show and come see it."

Hailey's eyes narrowed. "This is your only warning."

For the rest of the day, like a feather tickling my ear, a question distracted me.

It was a question about the movies I watched as a little girl, long before I started cosplaying with Dad. The villains are usually evil queens or witches. At the end, the heroine gets the prince—plus wildlife companions, or servants who conveniently doubled as appliances. She always gets more than just her true love; she wins friends, too. The losers end up alone.

Boy-stories are different, I've noticed. At the end, dragons are vanquished, and the hero gets the gold—and the girl, but only if he wants her.

Why do boys fight dragons and girls fight each other? In girl-stories, why is the fight always over relationships?

At lunch, I marched up to Hailey, Sydney, and the rest of the clique. I didn't sit down with them—just stood at their end of the table, careful to keep my tray of food carefully balanced.

"I don't care who wins the talent show," I announced. "I'm not trying to beat you."

"Good," Hailey laughed. "Because there's no way you can."

Sydney laughed next. "No one wants to see your stupid finger-paintings."

"We're not finger-painting!" I snapped, then cleared my throat and took a breath. "Look, I will not compete with you for the affections of others." Lifting my chin, I looked off into the middle-distance, a classic cosplay pose. "And in that way, I have already won."

"Wow," Sydney said, talking slowly, as if I were a confused toddler. "You're going to win a competition that has judges because you don't care what anyone thinks."

"No," I said, frustrated. The delivery of my line had been spot-on. She didn't get it. "I have already won because I don't fight other girls for attention."

"I don't think you really understand how a talent show works," Lucy ventured. "The group with the most talent wins."

"Oh, that," I said airily. "Yeah, we have way more of that, too. And don't forget our secret weapon." Technically, if she knew we had a weapon it wouldn't be secret, but my mouth was moving too fast for my brain to catch up.

"What secret weapon?" Hailey said.

"Our teacher," I replied as I walked away. "Maybe you need to research who Mr. Westchester is before you decide how bad our paintings are going to be, because he's world-famous." I smiled at them over my shoulder. "We're going to get a lot of attention. When we step onstage, no one is going to care about your dance. Everyone's eyes will be on our paintings."

With that, I took my seat at the other end of the table with my real friends.

Tess and Joseph were staring at me.

"Lizbeth," said Tess solemnly, "what have you done?"

Art Club later that afternoon was tense.

"I can't believe you turned this into a competition," Tess said as she furiously swirled her brush across her paint pallet.

"Well, technically, it was already a competition," I pointed out. "And you're the one who wanted to win it! You're the one who made a big deal of Art Club in the first place. I thought you'd be happy that we're getting noticed."

Tess slammed her paintbrush down on her easel, making little splatters of watercolor leap into the air. "You think we're working hard because we want to beat Hailey's clique?"

"Um, yes. That was my impression."

"To me, winning doesn't mean beating other people," she said in a cold, lofty voice. "It means I get to make art and raise enough money so that everyone else can make art, too. And it means that my dad will see what I'm capable of."

Paul pulled out one earplug, staring at us. Joseph watched too. I glanced at Mr. Westchester to see how he was reacting to this.

"I want to save the art program," Mr. Westchester said. "But in this room, I want you to do brave, honest work. That's all."

I blew a big breath out from my cheeks, facing the canvas on the easel in front of me. Now that I had challenged my former potential lifelong best friend to a talent show showdown, I had zero creative energy.

My canvas was a white expanse of terror. I didn't even know how to start, much less win. I wasn't the old Lizbeth, and the new me had been a complete disaster. In fact, everything I had tried lately had failed.

Tess was looking at Mr. Westchester with a thoughtful expression. "Speaking of honesty," she said, "I've been reading about you online. You used to be famous. Your paintings sold for a ton of money. Why'd you stop?"

For a long moment I thought Mr. Westchester wouldn't answer her. But then he let out a slow exhale. "My dad is, or was, a heart surgeon. He always said I had a surgeon's hands. Delicate and strong, precise. But I felt more comfortable holding a paintbrush than a scalpel." He sounded sad. I remembered him saying sarcastically, on our first day of art class, *So if you don't have a talent, you might as well do art?* I wondered if his dad had actually believed that.

"I tried to be a doctor. I wanted my dad to be proud of me. But when I dropped out of med school, Dad stopped talking to me. He thought that would make me give up. Instead, it made me mad. I wanted to show him he was wrong. So I sold more paintings than any other artist my age."

"And then your father died," Joseph said, nodding solemnly. "At the hands of your rivals." I really had to get Joseph to try cosplay. He'd be a natural.

"No! He died of a stroke," Mr. Westchester said. "The body isn't meant to last forever, kids. The wheels are gonna come off the bus at some point."

"You still haven't told us why you're here," I said. Did facing a blank canvas day after day become too hard?

"Without him to fight, I just didn't have anything left to say as an artist." Mr. Westchester's half-smile made me wonder what he regretted more: the fights with his dad or walking away from what he loved.

"Keep going," I said. "Dig deeper. You said that if we become artists, we're artists for life. Are you still an artist, even if your dad isn't here?"

He was silent for a long moment. "Well, I still want to prove him wrong. I'm an adult and my dad is gone, but in here"—he tapped his chest—"we're still fighting. But I don't know if that made me an artist, or just angry. That's why I needed a break."

"Your dad never knew you," Tess softly said, her gaze far off. "You tried to tell him the only way you could." Her attention returned to Mr. Westchester. "If losing your dad is why you stopped painting, you need to find a reason to start again."

"All your fans are still out there," Paul said. "They'd buy your art."

"I wish that inspired me," Mr. Westchester said. "But what keeps me going right now is convincing you kids to pick up a brush." He ran his fingers along the edge of an unused sketchpad on his desk, his brows knitted. "Don't waste a minute of your life trying to prove yourself to someone else. Nobody else gets to decide who you are."

I stared at my canvas until Mr. Westchester said it was time for all of us to go home. He had to leave, too. Sliding our easels against the wall, we arranged white cloth covers over them. Then Mr. Westchester flipped the light switch and I watched the ghostly white disappointment disappear into darkness.

Tess went straight home without saying goodbye to me.

As I got my backpack from my locker, I overhead Paul and Joseph yelling at each other from inside the boys' restroom.

I edged closer in the hopes of deciphering what they were saying, but just then, they both stormed out and headed in opposite directions. As Joseph barreled down the hall toward me, I stepped into his path.

"What is going on?" I asked. He wouldn't look at me. "Joseph, you can trust me. I'm your friend." When our eyes met, he got it. We *were* friends. And not because I had been assigned to the pod.

Joseph set his jaw. "I'm gonna make my move."

"What do you mean?" I asked. "You forget that I'm new. I don't know the whole story."

Joseph glanced from side to side. "You know there's a group of older boys who harass me, right? Steal my lunch and all?"

I nodded.

"Well, it's getting worse. But they offered me a way out. I'm gonna take it."

"Which is?" I prompted.

He glared at me but I pursed my lips, waiting, until he sighed, his eyes closing.

"I have to fight Tommy's brother." His lower lip trembled.

Fear shot through my body. Instinctively I reached for his hand, as if I could keep him safe. His hand was freezing cold. I couldn't imagine how afraid he must be.

"Joseph, you have to tell an adult."

He jerked his hand away from mine. "If I do that, those guys will hurt me even worse."

"Then *I'll* tell someone!"

"Lizbeth. I know you want to help, okay? But you have to stay out of this." He looked at the floor, then back at me, running his hand through his hair. "I've been training with Paul. I can do this."

A wave of nausea passed over me. "Who are you trying to be, Joseph? You're not a cage fighter. You're an artist." I swallowed back the awful feeling that I was betraying him by telling him the truth. "If you're ever going to stop bullies, it's not going to be with your fists. You don't have to do this."

He held out his hands, cracking his knuckles. "Everything's under control," he said, like I hadn't said a word. "Now be a good egg, and scramble."

Racing down the hall, I checked Mr. Westchester's room first but he was already gone. No one was in the main office, either. I found my social sciences teacher, but in explaining the emergency I realized my fatal mistake. I had forgotten to ask where the fight was taking place. I couldn't help Joseph even if I wanted to.

I ran to the carpool lane to catch Mom before she started to wonder why I was so late.

As soon as I got in the car, I texted Tess.

ME: *I know you're mad at me about the talent show stuff, but this is important. Joseph's going to fight Tommy's brother. I don't know where, but it's happening tonight.*

TESS: *What?! I'll call him and talk him out of it.*

TESS: *Also, I'm not mad at you.*

TESS: *At least, I won't be for very long.*

A fraction of the tension in my body eased. I hadn't ruined everything. We were still friends.

Watching the clock on the car's dash, I couldn't stop my legs from jiggling. Mom asked, of course, but I just told her the truth. I was waiting for Tess to text me about a boy. She grinned and turned up the radio.

TESS: *Joseph's not answering his phone.*

ME: *We have to tell his mom!*

TESS: *But we don't know where he is! We don't even know if he went through with it. He might even be home by now. Telling his mom will only make everything worse. SHE WILL FREAK OUT.*

ME: *We can't just keep quiet and let him get hurt!*

TESS: *15 minutes. If we don't hear back from him, I'll have my dad call his mom. Feathers will hit the fan though.*

Thirteen minutes later, we got a series of fist-bump emojis from Joseph. And one smiley face.

That was it.

CHAPTER 16

Early Friday morning, Tess was pacing in front of Room 223, and her face lit up when she saw me.

"Have you seen Joseph?" we blurted out at the exact same time.

"Girls are so weird," Joseph said from behind us.

Whipping around, we shrieked and hugged him, hard. I pulled back, inspecting him for bruises, cuts, or broken bones. Tess grabbed his chin, squinting as she turned his face sideways. "They didn't break your nose, did they?"

He grinned. "They didn't lay a hand on me."

"How?" I gasped. Lacing his fingers together, he stretched out his arms, cracking his knuckles. "I showed up yesterday after school, right? There they were. All of them. Extras, even. They brought extra eighth grade guys, no kidding. I walked up to them and said I was done being bullied by them. I wasn't going to take it anymore." He folded his arms.

"And then what happened?" Tess asked, breathless.

His eyes narrowed. "I think they could tell I'd been training. They didn't want to fight me. They backed off."

We filed into homeroom, ignoring the menacing looks from Hailey and her clique. The drama about winning the talent show seemed ridiculously petty compared to seeing a friend come so close to real violence.

It wasn't until after the tardy bell rang that I realized Paul wasn't here.

An uneasy feeling fluttered around in my stomach. I didn't say anything, though, because I didn't want to ruin the mood. Joseph was so happy, so confident. He was like a whole new kid. His eyes were shiny and his grin was a mile wide. Tess couldn't stop sneaking peeks at him, smiling wildly every time. They had lived as heroes in their imaginary worlds for so long. He was the first to prove they could be heroes in the real world, too.

I looked to my left at Paul's empty desk. It was neat inside, the notebooks carefully stacked, pencils and pens to one side. He liked order. A place for everything and everything in its place. He knew how things had to be done. Like helping people who couldn't help themselves.

A cold lump forming in my throat, I raised my hand. I told Ms. Farris I had to go to the nurse's office right away. It was an emergency.

"Faster, Dad."

"I'm driving as fast as I should," Dad said. "Why'd you tell me you had a bad case of turtle turds, anyway?"

"That's the family code word!" I gasped. "You didn't remember? Do you know how hard that was to say in front of the nurse? Geez, Dad."

I tried to breathe steadily and calm my nerves. Dark clouds were moving across the sky, fast. A bad storm was coming.

"All right, sorry," Dad said. "I forgot. But you made the right choice calling me."

"Well, you can take off from work easier than Mom." I glanced out the window, then forced myself to look at Dad. "Paul's my friend. I need him to be okay."

Dad glanced at me, and I knew he understood.

Minutes later, I rang the doorbell at Paul's house and waited.

For ages.

Thunder rumbled overhead. I rang the bell again.

Finally, Paul cracked the door open, his hair hanging down over one eye. "My dad's asleep," he said quietly. "He has a lot of trouble sleeping, so . . . could you come back another time?"

Instead of answering, I reached out and gently pushed his hair back, just enough to see if I was right. I heard Dad suck in his breath.

"Can my dad and I come in for a minute?" I asked. "We'll be quiet so we don't disturb your dad." I was pretty sure Paul had only answered the door to keep us from ringing the doorbell a million times.

Paul sighed, stepped back, and opened the door wider. Tentatively, I walked into the living room, Dad just behind me. The recliner was empty, so I figured Paul's dad was in his bedroom.

Paul's right cheek, directly underneath the eye, was swollen and bruised. His lower lip was split. His breathing was rapid and shallow, as if the pain was worse than it looked.

"You let those boys beat you up," I said. It wasn't a question. "You took Joseph's place."

He nodded. "I needed to buy him some time. So I struck my own deal."

"You'd be their punching bag if they left Joseph alone?"

"Pretty much. I promised not to fight back, and *they* promised that would be the end of it."

There was no doubt in my mind that Paul could've fought those guys off and come away without a scratch. Instead, he'd allowed himself to get pummeled. I wished Joseph could see what I was seeing now. It wasn't Paul's size that made him brave; it was his heart.

"Does anyone else know about this?" Dad asked. Lightning split the sky outside, visible through the windows on either side of the door.

"No, sir." Paul shook his head. "And we have to keep it that way."

"Son, you've got to tell someone. One of your teachers, or better yet, the principal."

"No." Paul stood straighter and brushed the hair out of his eyes, looking right at Dad. His bruises made me wince. "Those guys won't bother Joseph again." Paul's voice was hoarse.

"But they will hurt someone else," Dad replied, meeting Paul's gaze. "Someone who isn't lucky enough to have a friend like you."

"My dad's right," I said. "Paul, if we don't do something, they'll just pick another kid to bully."

Paul looked at me for a long time, and in his eyes I could read a history of pain. "I can't go to the principal and tell her I was in a fight," he said. "Even though I didn't hurt anyone, I'll be the one who gets punished. She'll just assume I started it."

"But why would—" I started.

"People say my family is trashy. They expect me to cause trouble."

My dad and I waited, sensing he had more to say.

Paul stared at the floor for a moment before continuing. "My dad used to work in construction, but he got hurt in an accident last year. He applied for disability, but something got messed up with the paperwork and he got denied. People think he doesn't want to work, but he does, more than anything. He just can't. Eventually he gave up trying to convince people about that." He tried to clear his throat but winced again. "Once people label you, you're stuck."

I felt like someone had poured cold mud down

my throat. I was lost for a moment, just looking at him, holding his gaze, thinking of what he had been through and who he really was.

How could someone so tough make me feel so mushy? My heart beat a little faster, too. Not from the swoony kind of love. I didn't know what other kinds there were, but this felt strong and reassuring, like when you're going downstairs in the dark and your hand finds the handrail.

"Ever since my dad's accident, I've been late to school a bunch of times and I've been really tired in class, because I do a lot around the house—helping my dad out, taking care of things my mom doesn't have time for because she has to work so much."

Paul licked his lips, wincing when he touched the open cut.

"I got in-school suspension three times last year, twice for being tardy so often, and once because I was so tired that I tripped and fell into another kid, who thought I did it on purpose. You ever notice that people assume big guys are bad guys? I can't risk getting expelled for this fight."

"But if you didn't fight back, it wasn't even a fight!" I exclaimed. "You could explain to Ms. Camp. I'll go with you. I'll back you up."

Paul shook his head. "It's fine, Lizbeth. I solved Joseph's problem. And I'll be all healed up soon—that's the least of my worries." He sighed and murmured, more to himself than to us, "What I really need is someone who can help my dad."

Heavy raindrops splattered against the roof.

"Can you excuse me for a minute?" Dad asked after a long moment. He walked toward the door, grabbing his cell phone from his pocket. The raindrops were landing faster and faster. Dad held his jacket over his head as he hustled outside to the car. He left the door open behind him and a cold wind swept in.

"Joseph thinks he stood up to those bullies and now they're afraid of him because he's so tough," I said.

"It should stay that way," said Paul. "Joseph needs to believe in himself."

I reached and touched Paul's arm. "Paul, you've been the real hero all along. You're the best of us."

"Nah." Paul scratched his head gingerly, and I wondered if there were cuts on his scalp, too. "Truth is, I realized too late that I taught Joseph all the wrong stuff. I focused on teaching him how to fight with his fists, but then I realized . . . my dad is the strongest fighter I know. And he can't even stand up."

Dad jogged back to us, putting his cell phone away. Wet hair was plastered against the sides of his face. "I just made a call to someone who should be able to help your dad reapply for disability benefits. I know that won't make all your family's problems magically vanish, but I'm hoping it'll be a place to start."

I couldn't believe my Dad was so calm and confident, so determined to help. I leaned my head against his arm for a second, trying to thank him without words.

"Paul," he went on solemnly, "if you want to change the way people see you and your family, that's all the more reason to get the school administration involved in this. I know it's scary, but you don't have to face everything on your own."

Gently, he rested one hand on Paul's shoulder. "You are not alone. Trust me?" I thought about that night so many years ago, when my dad had been a little boy, heartbroken and terrified and alone in the dark. No one had come for him. But here he was now, showing up for Paul. Showing up for me. Making sure that we weren't alone in the dark.

Paul looked at me before answering my dad. Did *I* trust Dad, after so much had happened between us?

I nodded and grabbed Dad's hand. Thunder cracked outside.

"I'll do it," Paul said.

"You're the most interesting friend I've ever had," I said Monday morning, swinging my legs as I sat on the bench outside Ms. Camp's office.

Paul cocked an eyebrow. "More interesting than Tess?"

"Well, it's a tie."

Dad had emailed Ms. Camp over the weekend, and we'd had an early morning meeting before school started. Paul and I had each told Ms. Camp what we knew about the bullying situation in general and, of course, Paul's faceoff with the eighth graders. She'd asked us to stick around afterward. Apparently, there were more meetings to come. Dad was still conferring with Ms. Camp and the school counselor behind closed doors.

Paul's legs touched the floor. Mine did not, which is why I swung my legs.

"Stop that," Paul hissed. "We're not at the park."

At that moment, several of the bullies arrived with their parents. I figured they were here for the next meeting. They didn't look at us or say anything, just stood around not talking to each other.

I felt like I should break the ice. "You may be encouraged to know that high doses of fish oil show promise in treating aggression. I read that on the internet."

A mother grabbed her son by the elbow and pushed him ahead of her into the office, glaring at me over her shoulder. Like I was the one with the problem.

Tommy and his older brother, Blake, showed up with their parents. Blake had a huge white bandage anchored across the bridge of his obviously broken nose.

I looked at Paul in confusion. "You said you didn't fight back!"

"I didn't!" he insisted. "I never touched any of them. I don't know who did that to Blake's nose." Blake's expression was as menacing and flat as ever, but Tommy seemed unusually subdued, refusing to look in our direction. My heart pounded fast. What was going on here?

Joseph arrived next with his mom in tow. The boys took a collective step back when he walked through the doors. This was a very different Joseph than the kid I'd met a few weeks ago—all strut and no slink.

My head spun.

Then Joseph saw Paul. His swagger faded away, but he didn't shrink in on himself. He just took in Paul's injuries with a serious expression. Neither of them spoke.

Ms. Camp opened the door to the office. "Good morning, everyone. I'd like to say I'm looking forward to this meeting, but that would be a lie."

"I received several emails this weekend," Ms. Camp began as we all crowded into her office, most of us trying not to accidentally brush up against each other. "Mr. Murphy contacted me with some concerns, as I've previously discussed with him. And the parents of these young men emailed me to report that *they* were victims of an assault on school property."

Joseph's mom scoffed loudly, then attempted to toss her poufy shoulder-length hair over her shoulder.

She had used so much hair spray it looked more like battle armor than a hairstyle.

I slid lower in my seat. Dad had insisted I stay, saying that I might have information on the "charges." I did not like the word "charges" in this context. I did not like anything about this. Blake's busted nose seemed to indicate that either Paul or Joseph had lied to me about how events had unfolded.

"Joseph, we'd like to hear from you now," Ms. Camp prompted.

Joseph remained unruffled. "Why not check the security cameras?" he said.

The bullies exchanged worried glances.

Joseph jabbed a finger at them. "These dummies let me pick where we met. And because they gave me advance notice, I hid emergency supplies."

"Where did this . . . meeting. . . . take place, Joseph?" Ms. Camp asked.

"By the cafeteria dumpsters, 4:30 p.m. Thursday."

Ms. Camp quietly conferred with the counselor, then grabbed a laptop and punched in a series of codes. A color image appeared on the screen.

Ms. Camp took in our shock at the quality of the video. "It's not bad, is it?" We saw live camera feeds on all the doors, the bus lanes, the carpool lane, even the trash dumpsters out back behind the cafeteria . . . and after a few more keystrokes, the footage on that square flew backwards. When the counselor froze it, we saw the bullies facing off with Joseph.

Ms. Camp's eyes lit with a new intensity. "Technology is a wonderful thing." Maybe hard evidence against these bullies was something she'd been wanting for a while, too. "My brother works for an outdoor video company. They donated the sports cameras and he set up the feed to run to my laptop. Oh, and here's what I really love." She tapped another button.

We had sound.

"You made a deal with me." Joseph's voice was clear. He was standing several yards away from Tommy, Blake, and the rest of the eighth-grade boys who had made life miserable for him—and for anyone else unlucky enough to be small, different, or facing hard times. "Don't you remember what the deal was?"

Smart. Joseph was trying to make them admit what they'd done.

The guys just stood there, arms crossed, muttering to each other under their breath.

"I guess you're dumber than you look," Joseph said, setting down his backpack and stepping closer to them. "You can't even tell me why I'm here."

"I'm going to beat you up," Blake said, bored, like he was talking about the weather. "Then the others will take turns pounding your face into the pavement."

"Except we won't, right, Blake?" Tommy said, sounding surprised.

"Listen, Tommy, Joseph *wants* me to beat him up. That changes everything. You want me to beat you up, don't you, Joseph?" Blake said. The other guys sneered, except for Tommy. Blake took a menacing step toward Joseph, who held his ground. Big drops of sweat sparkled on his forehead.

"I want you to leave me alone," Joseph shot back. "You said that if I let you beat me up, you'd stop bullying me."

"You can leave, Joseph," Tommy said. "Nothing's gonna happen. We're done here, okay?" Tommy pulled on Blake's arm and Blake shoved him backward.

"Tommy thinks you're a baby," Blake said. "But I don't. You know what I think?"

Blake took another step, and this time, Joseph

stepped back—glancing over his shoulder, careful where he stepped.

"You're nothing but a chicken," Blake said. He clucked, and his fists shot lightning-fast past Joseph's face. Joseph squealed and ducked just in time, causing the boys to roar with laughter.

"That's enough!' Tommy said. "You already got what you wanted, Blake. Let's go home."

"No way," Blake said. "I feel like having a little chicken for dinner."

The guys all began clucking and flapping their arms.

"I'm not a chicken!" Joseph yelled.

They only clucked more loudly.

Joseph looked at the bullies, eyes darting back and forth, as if calculating something. Then he flung his arms open wide and screamed: "I AM A SUPERCHICKEN!"

In a flash of motion, he reached for his backpack and unzipped it. He pulled out one egg after another, launching each missile with shocking accuracy at the boys' faces. The boys yelped, staggering, as yolks dripped from their noses, eyes, and ears. They furiously swiped at their faces, trying to clear the slick slime, but that only spread it further, entangling the oozy mess in their fingers. They shook their hands to fling off the slime, but it didn't work. It was like wrestling snot.

All of which left Joseph enough time to launch egg after egg. Finally, the bullies retreated.

Looking up to the security camera, Joseph flashed the sign of SuperChicken.

I stood up and cheered. My dad put a hand on my shoulder and gently pushed me back into my seat. Paul, sitting next to me, made a strange sound. After a moment I realized it was a laugh, coming from deep in his belly.

"Well," said Ms. Camp, "that does seem to clear things up. And it matches with what I've heard from other students." She nodded at Paul and me.

Joseph looked at Paul as he spoke to the bullies. "My friend Paul tried to take my place as your victim, but that wasn't enough for you. Then I bested you in a battle of wits, but that wasn't enough for you either. You still lied about everything and tried to get me in trouble."

"But . . . where did Blake get the broken nose?" Blake and Tommy's father demanded.

That's when I noticed that Tommy had tears running down his cheeks. When he looked up at his dad, his breath was coming in ragged gasps. "You always say a man is only as good as his word. And you should know that Blake is no good. He's no good, Dad!"

Blake's broken nose came from Tommy. Angered that Blake broke his promise to never bully Joseph again, Tommy had whacked his older brother with a water bottle on the way home.

Blake was probably going to be expelled, along with several of the other eighth-grade boys. While that got sorted out, I didn't think they were going to be at school. Joseph received just one day of in-school suspension, to be served after the talent show. Paul was cleared of any wrongdoing.

As we left the office, Joseph said to Paul, "It was really brave of you to have my back."

"Nah, enough about that," said Paul. "I've never seen anything more epic than that egg attack. Brilliant, man. Just brilliant. Where did you learn to throw like that?"

"I owe it all to SuperChicken." Joseph coolly shrugged, his walk still more saunter than slink. "All that work on the comics has given me incredible hand-eye coordination."

Seeing them walk down the hall together side by side made me break into a huge smile.

"Guess I'd better let you get to class," Dad said to me.

"Thanks for handling all of this, Dad." I wanted to ask him what that phone call had been about and how it was going to help Paul's family, but he was already hugging me.

"We'll talk more later," he promised, and I knew we would. In fact, the idea of going to a counselor and having a specific, regular time to talk was starting to grow on me. Maybe I could even make a list of things to talk about. Those holes inside us—the divorce, Dad's brother—might not seem so impossible to fill if we shared them more.

In homeroom, the class was really buzzing about the drama between the bullies and the Weirdos. A few people were on the side of the bullies, but everyone else sided with the Weirdos. It blended into talk of the talent show, making it seem like a very important us-versus-them showdown, instead of a group effort to do something good.

But at lunchtime, when we all walked to the

cafeteria, I noticed that both Joseph and Paul stood taller than usual. I got the impression that for the first time in their friendship, they also stood side by side as equals.

After school, Mom texted me that she was running late to pick me up, so I took my time heading to my locker. On my way there, I heard sniffles, so I detoured to investigate. Sydney was sitting on the risers in the empty music room, crying.

"Are you okay?" I asked.

She lifted her head from her hands and then glanced away. "Hailey is going to kick me out of the group if we don't win the talent show. Our rehearsals have been terrible."

Her eyes drifted back to me but quickly darted down again. "It's all my fault. I picked the song and routine. Now I don't know if we should switch songs, or change up the moves, or just practice more—there's no time!"

I rested my hand on her shoulder and she flinched. Embarrassed, I dropped it quickly. "I'm really sorry."

"You should be!" She wiped her eyes. "Thanks

to your art club, and the drama with the guys, Hailey thinks the talent show is basically life or death. She says we have to show everyone who the real cool kids are."

"Is there anything I can do to help?" I asked.

"Why would you try to help me?" She looked up at me, frowning. "I've been terrible to you."

"But I get it now," I said, sitting next to her on the risers. "You have to earn your place in that clique. And not just once. You have to earn it every single day."

She nodded, her chin trembling. "They're not going to forgive me for this, LivesW—I mean, Lizbeth. I won't have any friends. I won't even have an act for the show."

"It's mandatory," I said, politely ignoring that she'd almost called me by that rotten nickname. "You have to be in the show."

"No one can fit me into their act so late!" she wailed. "Don't you get it? If I don't make this dance amazing, Hailey is going to ruin my entire life."

My heart hurt for her. I had real friends, but I knew how hard it was to have fake friends. In fact, from the way Hailey had sometimes looked at Tess and Joseph, I suspected even she knew, deep down, that her clique was missing out on something better. Though that clearly hadn't stopped her from putting Sydney in this awful position.

Biting my lip, I thought about what the pod would say, what Mr. Westchester would want, and I made my decision.

"Don't worry, okay? I have a plan."

CHAPTER 17

Mr. Westchester was gone for the day, but he'd left his room open.

"Right in here, c'mon," I said, urging Sydney to follow me.

Hesitantly, she poked her head into the art room. "Are you sure about this?"

"I've never been surer of anything!" I grabbed a blank canvas from the supply closet and set it on the table for her. "Mr. Westchester is a great teacher, too, so he can show you what to do, and we can all help you."

Wrapping her arms around herself, she chewed her lip for a few seconds. "I just don't know if I can do it. I'm not an artist, not like you and your friends."

My heart glowed.

"Maybe you could show me what you're working

on?" she asked, her voice a tiny bit encouraging.

Great minds do indeed think alike! I was already at my easel "Look, this is mine." I lifted the cover and showed her the canvas. "See, it's still almost entirely blank."

"That's the 'stunning original work' you're entering into the show?" she asked, one eyebrow raised.

"No. I mean, yes, it will be," I replied, heat coming into my cheeks. "I'm just trying to show you that we're not ready, either. You still have time to make your own self-portrait and join our group."

Sydney's phone chirped. "My mom's here. Gotta go."

"Think about it, okay?" I called after her.

"I will, I promise," she answered.

As I left the art room, I realized I'd left my language arts notebook in my desk, so I jogged down the hall, praying Ms. Farris hadn't locked her classroom door when she left.

The door stood open and I was surprised to see her at her desk, sipping a cup of tea. A red pencil was in her hand, poised over a stack of papers.

"Lizbeth." She knew my name! She even said it without any trace of weariness or resentment in her voice. I wondered if she was feeling okay. "Let me guess. You forgot something?"

I just nodded, unable to meet her gaze, then rushed over to my pod and shoved my book in my backpack.

"Can you come over here?" She sounded almost human.

I shuffled over to her desk and got the courage to look up. Her eyes were green. I had never noticed before. I had only paid attention to the dark circles beneath them.

"You've stayed out of trouble several days in a row, despite a lot of drama going on around you. I'm impressed."

I stared at her, speechless.

She held out her hand. "Your name tag, please. You don't need to wear it anymore."

It was barely hanging on anyway, but I peeled it all the way off and crumpled it, then dropped it in her hand. "Thanks."

"I think I can recall your name now. In fact, I may never forget it." She laughed. "Did you know I had a baby four months ago? She's had colic almost the whole time. But my mother came to stay over this weekend. I finally got some sleep."

I knew she had a new baby, but I hadn't considered how this might be affecting her. "Oh. I'm glad. It must be hard to teach when you're exhausted."

"It's hard to do anything when you're exhausted." She took a sip of tea, then set the cup down. "I owe you an apology, Lizbeth. I was snippy with you when you arrived. I had very little patience. And I'm sorry."

"Apology accepted." I felt a sudden surge of curiosity. "Which was harder to deal with—the crying or not knowing *why* she cried?"

"Huh." Ms. Farris took a deep breath, and then exhaled. "That's a good question. The crying was intense for sure. But not knowing the reason for it, that was hard too. I thought if I could just put a name on it, I'd know how to fix it."

Something deep in my heart rumbled, like a heavy stone lifting and turning over.

For some reason my mind zoomed back to an old religious story about the very first man on Earth. The first thing the guy did when he realized he was in a new place was start naming the animals. That might seem logical, because animals needed names, right? No! They didn't need names. Animals don't care if they have names or labels or scientific classifications.

The man needed them. He was in a new place and maybe he was scared.

"See you tomorrow, Lizbeth with a *Z* and no *E*."

I grinned. "See you tomorrow. I'm glad you're finally sleeping. I had no idea you were nice."

Tuesday morning, Ms. Camp announced over the intercom that a reporter from the local newspaper was coming to the talent show to do a story about Art Club. Hailey glowered at me from across the room.

I tried to catch Sydney's attention, but she kept ducking her head to avoid my gaze. I really wanted her to join our group. Now I worried she had lost her nerve.

"Please remind your families to come out to the show in support of all our talented students—including our enterprising Art Club members!" Ms. Camp continued. "This is going to be the biggest talent show in Viper history!"

Was I the only one who thought Vipers weren't the most encouraging mascot?

❦

Sydney didn't come to Art Club that afternoon. I kept checking the door, hoping to see her walk through it, but she didn't. Concentrating on my self-portrait was hard when I was so distracted. I wasn't getting much done.

Without warning, Tess snapped. With one arm, she swept her canvas off her easel onto the floor. We all gasped as Joseph lunged to save it. He grabbed it and, as gently as if it were a kitten, set it on the nearest table, face up.

We inhaled sharply as if on cue. Her work was dazzling. In most ways, the painting looked like her—except for her eyes. Her eyes were huge, and inside them were reflections of everyone she loved. Us, her dad . . . and a blank spot, as if someone had been Photoshopped out of her pupil.

"Tess, what's wrong?" I said, my voice barely above a whisper. "That looks great."

"It's a mess," Tess grumbled. "I don't want to work on it anymore. I thought I was going to show my dad who I really was, and he would love it, but I can't even explain it."

"You'll figure it out," Joseph urged. "You'll get it right."

"Your painting is amazing," Paul said.

"No, it's not. It's dumb. It's even dumber than SuperChicken!" Tess reached for her backpack. She was done.

"Hey!" said Joseph in the loudest voice I'd ever heard him use.

Tess froze.

"SuperChicken is more than a comic, Tess. It's a philosophy." Joseph spoke with a confidence that stopped all of us from moving or saying anything else. "It's a belief that there can always be a surprise ending that nobody expects, not even us. When I flash the sign of SuperChicken, I'm not saying I believe in him. I'm saying I believe in you."

Tess wasn't smiling, but she seemed calmer.

I glanced at my canvas, wondering if Joseph would have a pep talk for me.

"You need to consider the possibility that you've finished the painting, Tess," Mr. Westchester said.

Joseph's mouth fell open. "It can't be finished! She doesn't like it yet!"

"Maybe it's more complicated than that," Paul suggested. He smiled, which I'd rarely seen him do, and reached for Tess's hand. Tentatively, she extended her hand and allowed him to hold it. I frowned, then caught myself and cleared my throat.

"We're the least popular kids in school," Paul said. "Starting self-portraits, knowing we'd have to display them at the talent show, that was hard. Maybe stopping them will be even harder."

I wondered if that was why Sydney hadn't shown up. Maybe it was easier for her to stay in a fake friendship than to risk embarrassment with real friends. Right now, staring at our canvases, knowing the entire community was going to see them, I kind of almost agreed.

Joseph's hand shot forward, resting on top of Tess's and Paul's, making a stack of three friends. "At least we're all in this together," he said. "I have your backs."

I placed my hand on his, completing the stack. "And I have everything else." No one giggled. These people still did not get me, not entirely.

"One for all and all for none!" Joseph yelled. Tess cheered.

Paul caught my eye.

I pressed my lips together so I wouldn't laugh.

"You should do a self-portrait, too," Paul said to Mr. Westchester.

Mr. Westchester shook his head.

"You're not afraid to try, are you?" I asked.

"I'm afraid of children," he replied, picking up a rubber band and aiming it at me.

I didn't flinch as it sailed over my head. "I hope you paint better than you aim."

"I'm not bad as a painter." He laughed and picked up a pencil, twirling it around his fingers. "I thought teaching art would cure me of ever wanting to do it again. I didn't count on you four, though."

As we worked, Mr. Westchester walked us through the plan for the talent show tomorrow. His plan was simple. How disappointing.

Ms. Camp and Mr. Westchester would unveil each painting while we stood beside it. We would each have thirty seconds to introduce ourselves and our work. The newspaper reporter might take individual pictures of us onstage, but after the show, we would do a group picture while the judges conferred—before the winner was announced and refreshments were served.

Tess, Paul, and Joseph were done with their

portraits. One by one, they slid their easels against the wall, arranged the cloth covers over their canvases, rested their hands on my shoulders, and left the classroom. Mr. Westchester looked up from his desk, nodding at them as they went home.

"I need extra time," I told him.

"Want me to call your mom?" Mr. Westchester asked.

"She's still at work but I'll text her. Can you stay?"

"No problem." He grabbed a sketch pad. "Maybe I'll try to create something too. Not for the show, though. That's your night. Holler if you need anything." He slipped earbuds in, propped his feet on the desk, and started making rabbit-fast pencil marks across the paper.

Alone with my canvas, surrounded by paints and brushes, I had to create myself.

Dad's nose. Mom's eyes. My heart, in dented and scattered pieces. For two years, I'd been trying to glue all the broken pieces of my life back together. Nothing had held. Suddenly, looking at the paints and palettes around me, I understood what I needed to do.

I had to blend.

Once you blend two things, you've made something new, something permanent. Just like I could never separate blue and red out of purple, nothing in my life could ever unmake me.

I mixed colors that made my heart sing, and when I had created a rainbow to choose from, I painted a picture of the true me.

My hair was a long bank of clouds that ran off the canvas. My eyes were huge and gold like the sun. My heart was going to be a big red supernova. Nobody would really understand what they were looking at when they saw me but I couldn't wait to tell them. Wasn't that what real life was like, too?

The paints were thick fluid and I dipped my brushes in and out of cups of water. Drips and dribbles fell everywhere and I knew Mom would grumble if I wasn't more careful to avoid stains. Creating was a messy business.

The clock ticked loudly, urging me to hurry. I couldn't stay here much longer.

There would be no finishing this, though, not really. That was why it was so hard to stop, and hard to think about showing it to others.

After a few more daubs of paint, I set the brush down. Mom would be here any minute. Somehow, looking at the portrait, I knew that everything was going to be okay. It was unfinished and imperfect, like everyone and everything. But there was nothing else to add that felt right. Whatever came next was still a mystery, even to me.

"Ready for me to cover it and put it in your spot?" Mr. Westchester asked. I nodded, a tight lump in my throat.

Kissing my palm, I blew a little imaginary fairy dust to myself and left.

I was alone in the restroom washing up when Sydney, Hailey, and their entire dance group entered. They must've been doing one final rehearsal in the music room. The temperature instantly dropped ten degrees, and their laughter and chatter turned to wide eyes and whispers. The girls circled around my mirror, avoiding any accidental contact as they moved past me.

"How are you doing, Sydney?" I asked, keeping my eyes on the mirror, watching her reflection.

"I'm good," she squeaked. Her smile was thin and tight, and she was careful to avoid eye contact.

Was she okay, really? I felt so bad for her.

Hailey set a package of makeup wipes on the counter and pulled one free. She dabbed at the glitter on her cheekbones. The only sound in the room was running water.

I scrubbed at the paint stuck between my fingers and under my nails. "Doesn't anyone in your group talk?" I finally asked.

They all glanced at each other. "What do you want to talk about, LivesWet?" Lucy asked.

"My name is Lizbeth!" I snapped, turning to face her and the other girls. "I wore that stupid name tag for weeks. Do you know how embarrassing that was? And you all made it so much harder for me!"

"Calm down," Hailey said, barely registering my distress as she looked at herself and posed in the mirror.

I took a deep breath. "I tried really hard to be your friend. You could at least use my real name." I grabbed a paper towel to dry my hands.

The girls all exchanged more looks and giggles. They acted like I couldn't see them. Fine, I could do that, too.

"Sydney, you still have time to join our group," I said, even though I didn't think she really could. I had to try one last time to help her get out of this clique. "We'll find something for you to do. Anything has got to be better than hanging out with these girls."

Her eyes darted at Hailey, who smirked. "That's okay," Sydney said, quickly looking back down. "I have a feeling everything is going to work out. I appreciate everything you've done, though. Honest."

Another girl choked on a laugh, but I didn't know what was funny. Maybe it didn't matter. Sydney had made her choice.

Grabbing the door, I flung it open and stormed out. The long slow wheeze as the restroom door closed behind me ruined my dramatic exit.

CHAPTER 18

Mr. Westchester was in a violent struggle with his tie. My hands were shaking so hard that I couldn't have helped him even if he'd asked. Tess and Joseph stood like stone gargoyles, expressions frozen in terror as we waited just outside the gym. Our paintings were already inside, in the stage wings. Mr. Westchester had been very careful to keep them covered so the surprise wouldn' be ruined for anyone.

Paul wasn't here yet.

"Remind me again what to do," Tess groaned. She was pale, worse than flu-pale.

"We'll sit near the front, all of us together," Mr. Westchester said in a monotone. I suspected he had rehashed this repeatedly with Tess. "Your group will go last. You'll all stand onstage together. Ms. Camp and I will bring out the paintings on their easels, with their cloth covers on. I'll give a short but enchanting speech on the importance of the fine arts and how Art Club was founded by four exceptional students, students brave enough to reveal stunningly honest self-portraits to the world."

Paul walked in, one earbud in his ear. I noticed his jaw flexing as he approached us. He was nervous, too.

"When Ms. Camp pulls the cover off your work," Mr. Westchester continued, "you'll each give your thirty-second speech. Then, as a group, you'll take your bows and leave the stage."

Moments later, we marched single file into the gym and took our seats in one of the cramped rows of folding chairs that had been set up facing the stage. The place was packed. Of course, that made sense—all the students had to be here, and most of them had brought family members. But some quick mental math revealed a surprisingly disproportionate adult-to-student ratio. Either some of my classmates had roped in every relative they had, or plenty of random community members had shown up.

Tess's press release in the paper must've worked. People actually cared about the arts. Or did they care about kids? Or both? My thoughts raced.

I was up to my ears in panic. I tried to hold my head high to keep from drowning in it. I had never faced an audience this size, even at cons.

The others were craning their necks, scanning the audience behind us for familiar faces. Tess's face brightened so I knew her dad was here. Joseph gave a sly tough-guy nod to his mom. Paul waved to someone. I followed his gaze, expecting to catch a glimpse of his mom and maybe even his dad—and saw it. Her. Claire.

My head whipped back around. "Did you just wave to that woman?"

Paul glanced behind again and Claire waved at me this time. "Ms. Johnston? Yes. She's amazing. Your dad put her in touch with my parents, and she got my dad's disability paperwork all sorted out, for free. She even came to our house so my dad would be comfortable during the meeting."

So Claire was the person my dad had called to help Paul. It made sense, since she was an attorney. Also, I had not known she used a last name. Scientific classification for cockroaches does not include last names. She was always ahead of me. I hadn't even identified her species. To my knowledge, she was the first of her kind.

"That's great," I replied weakly. "I'm glad she could help." I sneaked another glance, then hacked so hard that Tess pounded me on the back until I could breathe again. Claire wasn't just here—she was sitting with Mom and Dad, like they were all friends. What was wrong with them?

The lights dimmed as the first act took the stage.

Marcos was first with his sawing-his-sister-in-half routine. I already knew that Marcos had two sisters who were twins, so I had an idea of how the trick would work. Still, I was drawn in by the performance. Onstage, one of his sisters pranced around for the audience before getting inside the box and lying down. When Marcos sawed the box in two, each twin was actually in her own separate box. One pushed her head through to smile for the audience while the other pushed her feet through. The audience gasped as Marcos pretended to hit a snag and the first twin screamed.

Now I kind of wanted at least one sibling. It'd be cool to have someone to stuff in a box. Perhaps that would be the silver lining to both of my parents moving on with their love lives. I couldn't think about that too hard right now, though, since I was already trying not to hurl.

More acts followed, including the garage bands, singing, assorted dancing, and even the armpit farts. Those were surprisingly impressive, and the boys wore tuxedos with the armpits cut out. A seventh-grader accompanied them on violin, and I was convinced they were the frontrunners to win.

The butterflies in my stomach grew more frantic with every passing minute.

Hailey's clique was the second-to-last act. I watched in dread and horror as they danced. Their routine was . . . stunning. They deserved the word we had used in our announcement. They even got a standing ovation. Hailey made a point of looking right at me as she took her bow. She and the other girls disappeared backstage, and the audience continued to murmur about their talent and charisma. I had been wrong about the armpit farts. Clearly, Hailey & Co. would win. They deserved to.

Now our turn had come. I was sweating intensely, even on my back. We walked up onto the stage, the last group of the evening, each of us standing next to our work, each of us with our whole hearts on the line. What had we been thinking? Self-portraits were not exciting. They didn't get gasps or standing ovations.

The newspaper reporter was right by the edge of the stage, snapping rapid-fire pictures with an actual camera. Ms. Camp held a microphone, saying ". . . and now Tess will describe her work," as Mr. Westchester threw back the cloth cover on Tess's painting.

"This is for you, Dad," Tess said into Ms. Camp's microphone. "I have no idea why it turned out like this." Everyone laughed, and I could see her dad applauding, with two hands, his phone nowhere in sight. Tess beamed and my heart swelled with happiness for her. Maybe together they could figure out the missing piece.

Joseph was next. His was a multimedia image featuring a photo of Bruce Lee above a typed quote from the legendary martial arts star: *Remember no man is really defeated unless he is discouraged.* Alongside that, Joseph had added a charcoal sketch of himself in front of the school, hands on hips like a superhero. In the background, above a painted Atlanta skyline, loomed SuperChicken.

"I made this because I realized it's a mistake to think we have to fight other people to feel better about ourselves," he told the audience. "Believing the worst about ourselves and each other—that's our real enemy. That's what we have to fight against, all of us, every day. This self-portrait shows the version of myself I can be when I win *that* fight."

His mom dabbed at her eyes and everyone applauded.

Paul was next. A hush fell on the audience as he loomed over his easel. When Mr. Westchester threw back the cloth, we saw a set of eyes. Paul had only painted his eyes, rimmed in different colors. If you squinted, you would see that the lines of the iris were fragments of poetry and song lyrics. The dark space in the pupil wasn't empty, like Tess's. It made me think of the inside of a church at night. He had hidden those words deep inside, and I knew few people in the audience would look carefully enough to recognize the beauty they were seeing.

I reached for Paul's hand just as he reached for mine, our easels providing cover so no one saw. When Ms. Camp held the microphone out to him, he just shook his head. She moved on to stand next to me.

My feet felt pinned to the floor. An electric current seemed to be running through my body. White dots danced around the edge of my vision as Mr. Westchester reached for the cloth that covered my work. A camera flash blinded me but I heard the audience gasp, and then Paul dropped my hand.

When my eyes adjusted, the first thing I saw were the faces of the audience, shocked, perplexed. Dad was frowning; Mom had her head pulled back and a hand covering her mouth.

No one applauded. Ms. Camp dropped the microphone to her side. Mr. Westchester's face was ghastly pale. Blinking, I looked at my portrait.

Someone had plastered it in name tags, just like the one I had worn until recently. Inside the white space of each one was a horrible word. LIVESWET, DOGFACE, WEIRDO, UGLY, LOSER, STUPID, TRASH, WANNABE, DUMMY, FAKE, DERANGED, UNWANTED, FAILURE, ANNOYING, REJECT . . . and many, many more. I hadn't realized there were so many things people could call me.

My body froze, as if shame had stapled my shoes to the stage floor.

Paul's face flushed. Tess, Joseph, and Mr. Westchester stood shocked and unmoving. Everyone else assumed *this* was my self-portrait.

No one would even think to look underneath.

A memory came back to me in a horrible, nauseating rush. This was my fault. I knew who had done it. I had shown Sydney exactly where I kept my canvas.

I heard a giggle and glanced to one side. Hailey, Sydney, and the girls in their clique were hiding in the wings, hands over mouths to muffle their amusement.

Suddenly Paul grabbed the microphone from Ms. Camp and raised his arm like he was going to smash the mic right through the portrait. Mr. Westchester stepped forward, but his arms hung at his sides, useless.

My eyes met Paul's. I shook my head helplessly. He couldn't destroy those labels without destroying my art.

That's what hurts most about getting bullied. Like it or not, it becomes a part of you. My canvas was lost under all that meanness and how would I ever get it back? After everything that had happened in my life, how would I get *me* back? The painting had been my effort to do that and now it was ruined.

I looked at Mr. Westchester, feeling betrayed. He had made art and self-expression sound so beautiful—and look what happened.

As Paul brought the microphone to his lips, there were no sounds in the room, not even the rustle of feet or the whimper of a baby. My chin trembled.

"Tell us about your portrait," Paul said, his voice

steady as his gaze. He stepped closer to me as he said it, so I didn't have to hold my ground alone.

"This isn't my work." That was all I could force out. My throat had swollen tight with tears.

"So you didn't write those name tags," he said. "Who did? And why?"

I scanned the audience. In the glare of the stage lights, the tears in my eyes blinded me. Blinking them away, I couldn't see anyone clearly except the judges in the front row, who seemed concerned, like I had created art that was too edgy for my age.

"I don't know," I squeaked, then cleared my throat for a second time, trying to hold on to my dignity for a split second longer. I wasn't even sure why that seemed important when I was standing next to a billboard advertising my social failure.

Behind me, Mr. Westchester cleared his throat. Was he crying a little too?

I knew he needed this night to be a success. So did Ms. Camp. And if I was going to keep making art with the three best friends I'd ever had, so did I.

I took the microphone from Paul, holding it with both hands to keep it steady. "My self-portrait is underneath all those labels." Standing a little straighter, I tried to speak slowly, stalling as the plan came together in my mind. "I want you to see me. But you can't, not until the labels are gone."

And now I had it. My plan.

"One donation, one label." I pointed to the audience. "A donation to our arts program, of however much you can afford to give, buys you one label that you can remove yourself."

Mr. Westchester smiled and Ms. Camp practically jumped up and down with excitement.

"If you were ever stuck with a label you didn't choose, you know how much that hurts," I said. "And kids get stuck with labels all the time. We need your help to get rid of them."

Mr. Westchester stood on my other side, flanking me. I handed the mic to him and noticed his eyes were rimmed with tears.

"We're seeing something extraordinarily inspiring tonight," Mr. Westchester said. "And I want to challenge each of you to destroy a label. Do it for the kid you used to be or for the kid you're raising now. No more labels."

A low murmur erupted in the audience. Families started getting up from their seats, talking rapidly and gesturing at the portrait. I could hear parents naming the labels they wanted to destroy—names they had been called once, maybe—and I heard kids confessing what names they got called at school.

Joseph rushed back to the stage—I hadn't even realized he had gone—with a trash can that he set down next to my easel. Tess dashed up beside him with a big empty cardboard box. She handed it to Mr. Westchester, who pulled a pen out of his pocket and wrote DONATIONS on the side. A line of adults—every one of them with cash in hand—was forming.

"Sing," I whispered to Paul. "While they peel the labels off. It will seem like part of the act."

"So people can make fun of that, too?" he replied, shaking his head.

"Paul . . ."

"I just want *one* thing I don't have to constantly defend."

"We're artists now, Paul," Joseph said. "We're only as safe as we are bold."

Paul looked flustered, but not angry. "Well . . . I know 'Here Comes the Sun' by the Beatles." His voice rose on the last syllable like it was a question. I nodded vigorously even though I had only the vaguest idea who they were.

He sang, without a mic, and every note seemed

to scrub away a little more of the hurt that was in the room. A few parents knew the lyrics and joined in, then some lady I'd never seen sat at the piano on the side of the stage and played along. I realized it was Ms. Mayweather, the music teacher, when some of the chorus kids stepped up and crowded around the piano. The armpit fart guys threw in a few notes of their own.

A mom dropped some money into the box as her little girl peeled off a label, threw it in the trash and then tried to return to her seat. I say "tried" because all the families were standing, filling the aisles between the folding chairs, making their way to the stage.

None of these people had forgotten the label they had once been stuck with. Every one of them was willing to pay to see it destroyed. And there was no way to guess which adult hated which label. The best-looking adults tore off some of the meanest names. No one even had to pause. They each knew exactly which one they wanted. Some people cried. Lots of people hugged.

Darien came up with a woman who must be his sister. With a solemn expression, he gave me our special handshake, then moved on to make his donation and peel off a label. His sister grinned and did the same. A moment later I spotted Ms. Farris holding her baby—and for the record, the baby was super cute. A little behind them was Ms. Tyler from the cafeteria, who winked at me.

Whispers from the wings caught my attention, and I saw Sydney and Hailey watching the audience, their eyes wide, their mouths hanging open. As if horrified, Hailey mouthed the word "Mom." I turned to see a taller version of Hailey approach the stage. She offered Mr. Westchester a twenty-dollar bill and then peeled off a label. She looked sideways, into the wings, and I knew she was making eye contact with Hailey.

Paul finished singing. The air in the room felt clean, like after a rainstorm. I wasn't as hurt as I had been a few minutes ago. Somehow, this was going to be okay.

I even smiled as I watched my classmates, who nearly levitated with energy, determined to get to the portrait and destroy the label they were currently stuck with. I heard their parents promising the label was going in the trash tonight, no matter what.

The trash can was filling faster than I would've believed possible. The donations were growing, too.

The newspaper reporter snapped so many pictures that she barely had time to pause and make notes.

Joseph and Tess grinned like lunatics and I laughed aloud. Paul smiled wider than I'd ever seen before.

"I can see your teeth," I said to him. "I've never seen them. They're nice."

"You've never seen my toes, should I take my shoes and socks off?" he shot back. "What about my rear end?"

Tess guffawed.

The final layer of name tags, the ones that touched the canvas, still remained. Everyone grew quiet as the delicate, final phase of the work began. People winced as if in physical pain as the labels pulled some of the paint away, damaging the image beneath. I couldn't watch as those last labels came off, because they took a piece of me with them.

As people continued slowly, carefully removing name tags, I found myself wanting to explain my portrait. A bit of my planned speech came back to me.

I took the microphone again. "If you look closely, you'll see my heart is in the shape of a supernova. A supernova is a dying star. But there's something cool about supernovas that you might not know.

Sometimes, there's so much energy trapped inside a dying star that a new star explodes into life. I'm starting to believe that can happen in our lives, too. I'm learning that when we're hurting the most, when life as we know it has fallen apart, something incredible can still happen."

At that moment, Sydney stepped out from the wings, her head down, as a woman from the audience approached the stage. My breath caught in my chest. The woman handed Sydney a crumpled dollar bill. Sydney walked past the portrait, straight up to me, and offered me the dollar.

"I don't have much money," she choked out. The tip of her nose had turned red and her eyes were bright. "But I'm sorry. This all happened because I told Hailey which portrait was yours. I wish I could take all the rest of the labels back."

Waves of sadness and happiness crashed into each other in my heart—the feeling adults call bittersweet. "You can't," I told her. "But we can still start over. I'm sorry I messed things up for you with Hailey."

Sydney sighed. "She'll get over it. Or she won't, I don't care anymore." She turned and dropped the money into the box and walked off the stage to join her mom.

My own mom hung back, her face beaming and her eyes brimming with tears. Dad was standing in line next to Claire, who had cash in her hand.

I looked back at the portrait, my stomach suddenly cold and heavy. Only one label remained.

Claire dropped her cash in the box and, looking right at me, walked to the portrait. She ran her fingertips along the edges of the picture. Then her fingers came to rest on the last label. She touched each of its corners before gently pulling it loose. She turned to me, her hand extended. In her palm was the crumpled label UNWANTED.

I couldn't look at her. I had given that label to her. If I took it now, I'd be letting go of my security blanket, my anger at her for existing.

I reached for the label. I looked up at Claire, fully intending to smile.

Oops.

Well, okay, I did manage to look her in the eye. Let's focus on the positive.

I threw the label in the trash. With that, we were free to start over.

CHAPTER 19

There were refreshments. Day-old cookies and watery punch in paper cups printed with dinosaurs and elephants, but that was better than the refreshments in Ms. Camp's office, which were just stale air and remorse.

Claire and Dad found me standing with Mom. We were in a huddle with my pod-mates and their guests, all trying to get to know each other.

Claire turned her head at an angle, leaning down to speak discreetly in my ear. "Are we ever going to be friends?"

"I doubt it. But thanks for the donation."

That made her laugh aloud, and then I laughed, too. I summoned all my remaining courage, surprised to find any left. "Claire, I'm sorry. I'm sorry for treating you like you were the problem."

Her eyes widened, but not with the suspicion I had expected. "Have you figured out what the real problem is, then?"

Scrunching my lips together, I squinted and looked away. "I've been reviewing the evidence. There is a slight chance it could be me. Every time trouble shows up, there I am, too."

Claire laughed again. "Your theory needs some work, kiddo. When you're ready to fine-tune it, lunch is on me."

I puffed out my cheeks in mock nausea.

"I won't forget about your lactose issue," she said. "I'll even let you pick the restaurant." She smiled at me. "And that doesn't mean we *have* to be friends."

"We're already past that," I replied. "We're almost family. Even if I don't like you yet."

"We're moving in the right direction," she said.

Then she turned to say something to Paul's dad, who was leaning heavily on a metal cane and holding Paul in a one-armed hug.

I decided that when I got home tonight, I'd start that list of things to talk to the counselor about. My dad would be first. Claire would be number two. I liked the way that sounded. Claire is a big number two.

Mom draped her arm around me. "You are my favorite human being. I've never been prouder of you."

I leaned my head against hers, so grateful that she was my mom. My heart felt so much better than it had earlier tonight, when the cover had been pulled from my portrait. Kindness was powerful magic.

Mom deserved a sprinkle of it, too. "Mom, I want you to have coffee with that guy from your office."

A smile twisted the side of her mouth. "What's your angle here?"

I tried to open my eyes wide enough that she could see all the way into my heart, so she'd know I was sincere. "I just want you to be happy. You deserve all the happily-ever-afters in the whole world."

She blinked a couple of times, and her eyes turned shiny. I wrapped my arms around her and when she wrapped hers back around me, I knew we had started a new story. I had a feeling we were both going to like this one.

The reporter interrupted us. "So, who goes together?" She waved her hands over the entire group. "For the picture—who goes with who?"

There was a big group of us, certainly: Paul and his parents, Joseph and his parents, Tess and her dad, plus Mom, Dad and Claire.

I spread my arms wide. "I think we all go with each other."

The armpit farts won. Hailey's jaw dropped when it was announced. I'd never seen her so angry. I felt a little twinge of joy.

The newspaper reporter dutifully took the winners' picture, but our portraits were all anyone could talk about. People had kept donating even after all the name tags defacing my self-portrait were gone. The money might not be enough to save the whole arts program all on its own, but it was definitely a step in the right direction.

One judge picked up her purse, then cast a final, grim glance at my portrait and all the wadded-up labels in the trash. She caught my eye and said curtly, "I don't approve of name-calling, young lady, not under any circumstances. That's why you didn't get my vote."

Paul and I looked at each other and burst into laughter. Some things hadn't changed. We were still completely misunderstood.

"You get my vote." Mr. Westchester walked up. "All four of you do."

I basked in his smile.

"So, will you start painting again now?" Paul asked.

"I think so." Mr. Westchester nodded. "Tonight I realized what's holding me back. I have a label that I need to deal with." He tapped his chest, then sauntered off. I couldn't wait to see what he painted. I couldn't wait to see what happened next with so many things.

For so long, all I'd wanted was my parents—my family—under one roof. Those plans hadn't worked out. But in a surprising way, now I had such a big family we'd never fit into one house. So in the end, I got way more than I ever asked for or imagined.

And no one could have planned that, not even me.

TACO NIGHT AT PAUL'S: THE RECIPES

Why not start your own Taco Night tradition?
With adult supervision, you can make these recipes.
They're simple, fast, and easy to adjust for dietary
needs. You can make gluten-free, vegetarian, and,
yes, dairy-free versions.

HOMEMADE TACO SEASONING

This is at least as tasty as any store-bought seasoning—plus there are no preservatives, strange-sounding chemicals, or "free-flow agents," which would surely make Lizbeth suspicious. You can also make big batches of this and give portions as gifts at the holidays.

INGREDIENTS:

4 tablespoons chili powder
2 tablespoons paprika ("smoked paprika" if you can find it)
2 tablespoons cumin
2 tablespoon garlic granules
2 tablespoon corn masa (corn flour, found in the international foods section of your grocer)
1 teaspoon chipotle powder
1 tablespoon dried oregano
1 tablespoon onion powder
1 teaspoon black pepper
1 teaspoon salt

INSTRUCTIONS:

1. Mix all ingredients and store in an airtight jar or baggie. If you prefer spicier seasoning, add more chipotle powder, up to one tablespoon per batch.

TACO MEAT

Serves 4-6. If you want to make a vegetarian taco, you can substitute plain canned lentils for ground meat and follow the same recipe. It will taste a bit different, but it will still be delicious.

INGREDIENTS:

1 tablespoon oil

1 onion, diced

1 pound ground beef or ground turkey

¼ cup homemade taco seasoning (add more later if you want!)

2 tablespoons tomato paste

1 teaspoon brown sugar

INSTRUCTIONS:

1. Heat 1 tablespoon oil in large skillet.
2. Add onion and stir over medium heat until onion begins to brown slightly at the edges.
3. Add meat and stir over medium heat until done. (For most meats, you want to hit at least 160 degrees F to be safe. You can use a food thermometer to check the temperature.)
4. Turn off heat and add tomato paste, brown sugar, and taco seasoning.
5. Stir well and serve.

RICE AND BEANS

This can be a fun side dish for a feast or a tasty, simple meal on its own. Serves 6.

INGREDIENTS:

1½ cup uncooked rice (you can use brown, long-grain white, or basmati rice)

2 cups water (or, for a richer flavor, use chicken broth or vegetable broth)

1 tablespoon butter (or oil)

1 tablespoon oil, preferably olive oil

1 onion, diced

2 teaspoon garlic granules or garlic powder

1 small bag frozen corn

1 14-oz can black or pinto beans

1 14-oz can fire-roasted diced tomatoes

1-2 tablespoons homemade taco seasoning (see recipe)

INSTRUCTIONS:

1. In a large pot with a lid, add rice and water (or chicken broth) plus one tablespoon butter or oil.
2. Bring water to a boil.
3. Stir, then reduce heat to low.
4. Cover the pot with a lid and allow to simmer for 20-25 minutes, or until rice has absorbed all the liquid and is soft.
5. While rice is cooking, prepare seasonings. In large skillet, heat 1 tablespoon oil and add diced onions.
6. Stir over medium heat until onions start to lightly brown at the edges.
7. Add the rest of the seasoning ingredients into skillet and gently stir.
8. When rice is done, add seasoning ingredients into rice pot and stir.

PICKLED JALAPEÑO QUESO

This is an Americanized take on Mexican hot cheese dishes. You can keep it simple or add extra ingredients to your version.

INGREDIENTS:

16 oz white American cheese (or dairy-free or lactose-free American-style slices)

1 10-oz can mild diced tomatoes and green chilies

¼ cup pickled diced jalapeños, with juice (Tess would want to add a lot more, but that's her style)

½ cup evaporated milk, whole milk, or almond milk

2-3 tablespoons chopped onion (optional)

2-3 tablespoons cooked chorizo crumbles (optional)

2-3 tablespoons fresh cilantro (optional)

INSTRUCTIONS:

1. Place ingredients in a microwave-safe bowl, a saucepan, or a slow cooker and melt over low heat.

2. Watch carefully and stir several times throughout the melting process.

3. Serve when cheese is melted and all ingredients are combined.

CHOCOLATE BAR CHIMICHANGAS

This recipe seems to have been pioneered by a Mexican restaurant called Pedro's decades ago, though it's hard to know for sure. You'll need toothpicks and a foil-lined cake pan with raised sides. The foil makes clean-up easy, and the cake pan keeps your oven clean in case of chocolate spills or leaks. Serves 4, although you may want to split yours with a friend!

INGREDIENTS:

4 full-size candy bars (Joseph uses Snickers)
4 burrito-sized flour tortillas
4 tablespoons melted butter
Ice cream and chocolate sauce

INSTRUCTIONS:

1. Preheat oven to 400 degrees.
2. Line cake pan with foil.
3. Place unwrapped candy bar in the center of a tortilla. Wrap tortilla up. Tuck edges under and secure with toothpicks. Place inside foil-lined cake pan with seam facing down.
4. Brush melted butter over each chimichanga.
5. Bake for 15-20 minutes, or until golden brown.
6. Serve hot with a scoop of ice cream and a drizzle of chocolate sauce.

ACKNOWLEDGMENTS

To my agent, Melissa Jeglinski: Thank you for everything you've done to get this book out into the world. I appreciated every step in the journey. To my editor, Amy Fitzgerald: I'm forever grateful this book found its way into your hands. Your whole focus is on serving the reader; what a privilege to write for you. Thank you to the whole Lerner team!

My family: Mitch, Lauren, James and Elise, plus Mom and Dad, Carey Lynn and Bob, who always encouraged me to keep going even when I lost my way and my mind (usually on the same day). Also thank you to Jim R, who provided much of the inspiration for the juvenile humor. I love him, but especially Louise. And thank you to Gidget and Marty, Tracie B, Stephanie L, Susan, Alissa, Jen, Linda, Jen and Steve, Whit and Tracy, Eric and Shari, and Sherry and Scott. Thank you to Taylor Scott at The Fish, who encourages millions of us every day while the world is trying to scribble on our name tag.

Thank you to Janice Hardy, who offered invaluable thoughts on the first draft. Stephanie Garrett and